THE GRAND
SEXTET

Get four, full-length ebooks – **BLOODY PARADISE, FROM ICE TO ASHES, TROPICAL ICE,** and **SING FOR THE DEAD** – and lots more exclusive content, all for *free!*

**Details at the end of
THE GRAND SEXTET**

SIX STUNNING SHORT STORIES

THE
GRAND
SEXTET

From the author of the Dean Wister Crime Series

DENNIS D. WILSON

Designer Credits
Cover art by **thecovercollection.com**

Interior design by **Anna Zubrytska**

Produced in the USA
Print 978-1-62134-437-7
E-Pub 978-1-62134-439-1
Mobi 978-1-62134-438-4

Published by Water Street Press
Healdsburg, California

For Gary Eckles

*I am honored to have shared your life's journey,
and will always cherish the memories of our
triumphs and tribulations.*

CONTENTS

ACKNOWLEDGMENTS

Thanks to Lynn Vannucci, my publisher, editor, and sensei. Her coaching, cajoling, and insightful criticism improve my writing every day.

THE GRAND TRIATHLON

Sheriff Danella Cody sipped her coffee and turned the page of the *Jackson Hole Daily News*. Her heart skipped at the first line of a story on page three, and for a moment she couldn't breathe. Rising from her seat to close her door, she spoke tersely to her assistant. "Joanie, hold my calls," she said, closing her eyes for a moment, hoping she'd somehow misread the headline. Finally, she opened her eyes, took a deep breath, and read the story.

Former Jackson Hole Guide Dies In Fall In Himalayas

Zamir Hussein, 46, died Tuesday from a fall while descending The Shark's Fin on the Meru Peak in India. His expedition was only the second to successfully summit the mountain. The first successful summit was led by Jackson resident Jimmy Chin and documented in the award-winning feature film *Meru*. Further details of the accident were not available at press time.

Dani closed her eyes again. She thought of Zamir fairly frequently, but she hadn't seen or spoken to him since that summer nearly twenty years ago. She considered it the pivotal summer of her life. She'd been tested and found qualities within herself she'd no idea she possessed. She'd discovered herself that summer, maturing physically, emotionally, sexually. She was a girl when she met him, only a year out of college. By the end of the summer, she'd become a strong, self-confident woman. Zamir had challenged her to accomplish impossible things, the first person in her life to have that kind of faith in her abilities. Not even her college basketball coach had shown that kind of faith in her. She looked at her bookshelf, at the framed picture of the two of them standing on the Grand Teton, each of them so sure it was one of the best days of their lives.

She got up from her desk and, on the way out of the building, muttered absently to Joanie, "I'm going to be out for a while. You can reach me on my cell if anything important comes up." She got in her four-by-four and started driving to Teton National Park, the place she'd first seen Zamir Hussein.

She'd been a rookie, and the only woman in the Teton County Sheriff's Department, when she met Zamir. She'd just completed her first year of duty, and it had been a rough twelve months. The hazing had been nearly intolerable from the men on the force. Not just the normal stuff that all rookies go through, it was as if they couldn't make up their minds about her. They would alternately hit on her, and then make crude comments insinuating she was a lesbian.

She had to admit she'd been a bit full of herself when she'd been hired on by the Sheriff. A local girl and renowned high-school athlete, she'd been the star forward on the University of Wyoming women's basketball team that had made it to the elite eight in the NCAA tournament, along the way upsetting number-one-seeded Tennessee. It was the farthest any Wyoming college team, men's or women's, had ever advanced in the tournament, and it was the biggest story in the state. Then, when she graduated and came home to take a job at the Sheriff's department, it made the front page of the *Jackson Hole Daily*, and the men on the force didn't appreciate the notoriety of the female hotshot rookie. The constant hazing her first year on the job had weakened her confidence and made her question her ability to succeed in such a male-dominated profession.

She met Zamir when she took a rock-climbing class. Although she'd been quite an athlete in high school and college, primarily as a swimmer and basketball star and, growing up in Jackson, had done a fair amount of backcountry hiking, she'd never had the time to explore rock climbing. It was a beautiful day in late May, and with the upper mountain still covered in snow fields, it was too early for most of the guided climbs the tourists loved, and too dangerous for the weekend warriors, so

Zamir was teaching rock-climbing classes at a lower cliff overlooking Jenny Lake. There were only four people in Dani's class and she quickly became fascinated with Zamir's exotic looks. He was about five-eight, eyes as black and as deep as an oil well, his hair pulled back in a man bun she wouldn't see again until the millennials made it popular over a decade later, and he had the wiry body of a jockey. He spoke perfect and somewhat formal English with an accent that she surmised to be Arabic or Middle Eastern. Later in the day, when he removed his shirt to demonstrate a particularly difficult move, she thought she could see every muscle outlined in the chestnut sheen of his back. He turned and caught her thinking just that. "Dani, come on up here and try this."

She'd been preoccupied surveying his athleticism and hadn't been paying close attention to the hand- and footholds, but she quickly scrambled up the fifteen feet or so to the ledge where he was standing. She clipped her harness into the line and looked at him.

"Go ahead," he said.

Dani took a tentative first step, then a handhold, followed by two diagonal moves up the cliff. Then she stopped.

"What's wrong?" said Zamir.

"I'm stuck. I can't find another hold. I can see one, but I can't reach it."

Zamir helped her down, and she felt humiliated. He had made it look so easy. "I'm glad you made that mistake, Dani." He was now addressing the entire class. "It's good that you made it there instead of a hundred feet up."

Dani looked up. "We are actually going all the way to the top?"

"Oh, yes. By the end of the day we will be looking over the edge."

Dani didn't think so, but kept quiet.

"There are two parts to developing into a good rock climber," Zamir said. "First there is technique, and second, and just as important, is being able to see the route so you don't climb yourself into a tough position. Now watch and pay attention to my route." In ten minutes he was at the top, setting the ropes in pitons along the way, and then he quickly belayed himself back to the bottom. "Who wants to go first?"

The other three members of the class looked at each other and one of them said "Ah…I don't think this is for us. But thanks." They removed their harnesses and walked away.

Zamir looked at Dani. "What about you?"

Dani didn't say anything but turned and scrambled up the route that Zamir had set, following the holds that Zamir had demonstrated. Zamir followed behind her and when they reached the top and looked down, she was exhilarated.

"Have you done any climbing before?"

"No, I haven't." Dani breathed heavily.

"Maybe in a gym?"

"No, this is my first time."

"In that case, you are a natural. I'm excited for you. You have great potential."

Zamir showed her a few more moves, and when the lesson was over, she was disappointed it had gone so quickly.

Later that day Dani sat at the bar at the Silver Dollar in Jackson, listening to the country band and sipping a Jack and diet Coke when she felt a man lean close to her ear and ask, "So, do you want to climb the Grand with me?"

She looked up and Zamir was flashing a blinding grin that seemingly took over his entire face. "Yeah, right," she laughed.

"No, I'm serious. I take up clients all the time with much less ability than you have. Give me a full day of lessons with you, and you'll be able to climb it for sure."

Dani wasn't as sure as he was. She knew the Grand Teton, at 13,770 feet, was one of North America's iconic climbs. She knew that dozens of tourists climbed with guides each summer. She also knew that every year, several people died climbing it. "I'll consider it," she said, more because she wanted to continue the conversation than any real inclination to make the climb.

That evening they talked, and listened to the music, and Zamir convinced her that he was serious about climbing the Grand, and they danced closely at closing time, and it didn't even bother her that she towered over him so that his head was on her chest. "Dani, I don't want this evening to end. Would you come back to my place?"

She considered for a moment. It'd been awhile since she'd been with a man, and maybe it was the fact that Zamir had treated her as an equal this evening, had actually been interested in what she had to say, which was such a contrast to the men on the force in the last year, and so she said yes.

"Can you drive?" asked Zamir. "My ride's at home. I hitched into town with a friend."

Zamir directed her to turn off about five miles outside of town on a gravel road that followed a creek. A few minutes later he directed her onto a narrow dirt road that led through a grove of cottonwood trees.

"We're here," he said.

"Where?" asked Dani.

"This is where I live." He pointed to a white Ford cargo van parked about a hundred feet from the creek.

"You have to be kidding," said Dani.

"It has everything I need," said Zamir. "Let me show you."

Against her better judgment, and possibly because alcohol influenced her decision-making, she let him take her into the van. She was surprised that it actually was very homey inside. It was equipped with a futon, a large cooler, built in shelves on one of the walls, and the opposite wall was lined with climbing equipment dangling from hooks like fish on trotlines. Everything was neatly organized and it did appear to meet her minimum hygiene requirements.

She sat on the futon, and Zamir offered her a drink. "Just water," she said, still not quite sure what she'd gotten herself into.

Zamir pulled two bottles of water from the cooler and sat next to her. "Look, I know this may seem a little strange to you, but for a climber this is pretty luxurious accommodations. I don't have a lot of money, and this allows me to spend all my free time here in Jackson climbing, which is what I'm here for this summer. I'm sure you know what it costs to live in this town."

Dani had grown up in Jackson. Her parents had been long-time residents in the valley and owned a cattle ranch. Although she hadn't ever personally experienced the realities of living hand-to-mouth, she had met plenty of people in town who had. "Don't worry, Zamir," she said. "This is fine. In fact, it's very cozy."

He surprised her again that night. She'd expected and was prepared for a sexual encounter. Instead, they cuddled on the futon and talked through the early hours of the morning. He was shocked when he learned what she did for a living. "And to think I was just about to offer you some weed."

"So where are you from, Zamir? You have an accent that I can't quite identify."

"I was born in Iraq. My father is a surgeon in Chicago. He came to America when I was a year old, and my mother and I were able to join him when I was nine. Most Americans figure I'm some kind of *A*-rab. I get those looks whenever I speak to people outside of the big cities, but my family are all citizens and proud of it." He had emphasized the "A" in *A*-rab, and Dani knew exactly what it meant when an American pronounced it that way.

They fell asleep while talking and, when she awoke, she didn't know where she was. When she remembered, she felt a little foolish for letting a strange man take her to his van in the middle of nowhere. So foolish she decided she wanted to leave, but as she was putting on her shoes and preparing to sneak away, Zamir asked, "Dani, where are you going? Don't leave yet, let me make you breakfast."

She looked up, and he was flashing the same blinding smile that he'd shown at the Silver Dollar the night before. They sat on a log next to the creek as the sun rose over the Tetons and sipped tea and ate day-old bagels with huckleberry jam. Dani looked up at the Grand and wondered if he was joking about taking her to the top. Maybe it was just a ruse to get her into bed. Then again, she'd been in what passed for his bed and he hadn't even tried anything.

"What are you thinking?" Zamir asked.

She looked at him and then up at the Grand. "Are we really going up?"

"Your next day off, we spend the day preparing you. And the day after that, we'll do the climb." And that's exactly what happened.

They slept together for the first time the evening after their climb, two weeks later, at Dani's apartment in downtown Jackson. She wasn't about to spend their first night together in a van. After that, she'd spent every off day the rest of the summer with Zamir, climbing, dancing at the bars in town, and making love. They climbed the Grand twice, and the other Teton Peaks as well – Owen, Moran, Teewinot, and Thor. They drove down to the Windriver Range and spent five days backpacking there, hiking twenty miles in and another twenty out to climb the tallest mountain in Wyoming, Gannett Peak. She felt her body change, her muscles became long and lean, and when she thought of the sheer granite faces she'd climbed – wedging her toes into the smallest of cracks and then stretching her six-foot body to pull herself up with her fingers, clutching a tiny crease in the rock – she was amazed. By the end of the summer, she felt strong, confident, and nearly invincible.

It had been a hot, dry summer that extended into September. She met Zamir for lunch on a clear, late Fall Monday. Through the smile he gave her, she could tell he had something to say. "So, I've been thinking… A couple of the guides did this unconventional Grand Teton Triathlon last week. And we've been doing a lot of climbing all summer, and we're both in pretty good shape, so I was wondering if you'd want to do it with me."

"Maybe. What do you mean *unconventional*?"

"It's sort of a made-up event by some of the guides. You bicycle from town square to Jenny Lake, which is twenty-one miles. Then you swim across Jenny Lake, which is one point three miles, of course we'd use wetsuits, it'd be hard to swim in that ice-cold mountain run off otherwise, then from the other side of the lake we hike the eight miles or so to the lower saddle, climb the Grand Teton, and then reverse the process. So it's a total of about forty-two miles biking, a little over two and a half miles swimming, and twenty miles or so hiking and climbing."

"And this is done all in one day?"

"Yeah, that's the idea. It should take fifteen or sixteen hours, so we'd leave from town square about three AM."

"And when would you like to do this?"

"I think you're off tomorrow, right? And the weather forecast looks really good. It's rare to be this warm and clear this time of the year."

Dani knew Zamir was leaving in a couple of weeks to climb in Argentina. They hadn't talked about what it would mean for their relationship. Dani had become very fond of Zamir, but neither of them had used the "L" word, and she didn't know if they had any future outside of this summer. This crazy triathlon could be a great way to cap off the season. A twenty-mile bike ride each way was nothing, she was a very strong swimmer, and she'd already climbed the Grand twice this summer… It sounded *very* challenging, but not impossible.

"I'll try it." She shrugged. "What about ferrying the climbing equipment across the lake?"

"Well, that's the other challenge," Zamir admitted. "We'd be taking only a water bottle and some power bars with us. This climb would be free solo."

Free solo. That meant no ropes, no belays, no safety net. She'd free soloed some smaller routes with Zamir this summer, but nothing like this. "Zamir, I'm not sure I'm ready to free solo the Grand."

"Dani, you are. Think about it. We used ropes both times that we climbed it this summer, but you never needed them, you never even came close to falling, and now you know the route extremely well. I'm sure you can do it. There is nothing like the focus on a free solo. It makes you feel truly alive."

Or truly dead, she thought. "Let me think about it." She looked at Zamir. He thought she could do it, but did she?

"I'm going to drop off a bag with some climbing clothes and food at the boat dock just in case you say yes." Zamir grinned. "And if we're going to do this, I want to go to bed early. I'll meet you at the town square."

Dani sat in her truck at the Jenny Lake overlook and gazed at the alpine lake and the blue granite Grand Teton rising above. Many of the details of their adventure that day were hazy in her mind but, as she sat there, flashes of that day came back to her in vivid images, as if she were sitting in a darkened cinema.

When she'd met Zamir at three AM in the town square it was a nippy forty-degree morning, but a full moon lit their way. Now a dedicated bike path paralleled the park road all the way from town to Jenny Lake, but then there had been no bike path, but also no traffic on the road at that hour, and their headlamps had been sufficient to supplement the moonlight. Zamir set a brisk but comfortable pace on the twenty-mile ride to the lake, but Dani was surprised at the steady incline of the road; she hadn't really noticed it before, and she was definitely sweating when they locked their bikes at the east side of the lake and changed into their wetsuits.

Jenny Lake is an alpine lake, several hundred feet deep, and the water is pure snowmelt. Even in late summer it is still ice cold. The one point three mile swim took around an hour, and they were changing into their climbing clothes by 5:30 AM for the eight-mile hike through switchbacks. There was 5000 feet of elevation gain from the boat dock to the lower saddle, which is where the climb to the peak begins. They arrived there around nine AM.

"We're making good time, Dani," Zamir told her. "This should get us to the summit by one or one-thirty."

Dani knew that it was important to summit before the typical afternoon thunderstorms hit the top of the mountain. Lighting loves the granite peaks, and you don't want to be at the top during a storm.

She remembered the climb up as uneventful. There weren't many guided trips after Labor Day, and so there weren't the queues of climbers near the summit that you find during the height of the season. Zamir was right – climbing without ropes did make her feel more alive and more focused. The biggest challenge in climbing the Grand Teton isn't the technical challenge if you're a competent climber, it's the exposure. There are places where you are on a ledge with nothing but thousands of feet of air below you, and without a rope it plays with your mind. Dani was surprised that she was able to ignore the exposure and focus on her route. They made good time and summited around one-thirty, took a picture, had a snack, rehydrated, and began their descent.

Dani knew the descent was actually more dangerous than the ascent. There is much less visibility on your hand- and footholds, and fatigue can become the fatal wild card. The exhilaration and adrenalin of the summit is gone, your body's reserves are depleted, and it's easy to lose concentration. Dani was acutely aware of this and consciously increased her focus. They were descending with Zamir ahead of Dani in the more difficult pitches, and then Dani moving ahead in the easier sections, when it happened. Dani had just stopped on a ledge as Zamir moved past her, and she saw a handhold crumble under his weight. He seemed to suspend himself in mid-air and she saw terror in his eyes as he started to fall. Instantly she wedged her foot in a crevice and reached out, able to grab hold of only his approach jacket with one hand. Zamir weighed a mere 130 pounds, but she was holding on to him with her arm strength only, leaning her body toward him, and she didn't know how long she could keep her grip until her foothold loosened. Zamir thrashed, desperately searching for handhold, for what seemed an eternity as Demi's arm burned, but in reality it was just a couple of seconds. His hand found a tiny crevice and he wedged his fist into it, then his foot found a toehold in the rock, he stabilized himself, and she felt his weight go off her arm. They both rested, breathing heavily, and looked at each other without speaking. They continued down the mountain deliberately, not speaking even when they were on solid ground, and hiking the rest of the way to the boat dock.

At the dock they changed back into their wetsuits. "Dani. You saved me up there. "

"We're on the home stretch now," she replied.

Halfway across the lake, Dani could see Zamir was losing his form and struggling. She swam close to him and said, "Let's flip on our backs and rest for a minute."

She set a slow, steady pace next to Zamir on the way back. When they arrived at their bikes and changed out of their wetsuits, Zamir didn't speak and Dani sensed that he was embarrassed. She'd been the steadier, stronger climber today, and the stronger swimmer. She was proud of that, but she felt badly for Zamir.

Compared to the rest of the Triathlon, the bike ride back to town was a piece of cake. Still, their bodies were exhausted, and they had to take a slow pace. They arrived at Town Square just under sixteen hours after they'd left. They climbed off their bikes and embraced. They'd done something that few had done before. The Grand Teton Triathlon wouldn't become a "thing" in the Tetons until over a decade later, when magazine articles started appearing about the challenge.

"I don't know about you, Dani, but I could use a beer and a burrito," said Zamir. "What to try the Cellar?"

The Cellar was a bar in the basement of an office building off town square, popular with climbers and skiers, and known for its humongous burritos. "Let's do it," said Dani. "But they have music on Tuesday nights, and it'll probably be packed."

"Probably," said Zamir. "But then we can brag about our exploits."

When they walked into the Cellar, they were shocked. It was nearly empty. There was no band, and only one person, an old man, sat at the bar, and he and the bartender were staring at the television over the bar. Dani and Zamir took a seat and looked at the scene on the TV. They sat for several minutes trying to process what they were seeing, a video from New York City earlier in the day.

As they watched, a jet flew into one of the World Trade Center towers, and then the scene changed to show the towers collapsing in a cloud of horrifying dust. No one spoke, and the video changed to a recording of President Bush addressing the nation.

Dani and Zamir looked at each other in shock, and the bartender turned to look at the two of them. He looked directly at Zamir and said, "I know you. You've been in here before, and I should have never put up with it. From now on, no *A*-rabs are served in this bar. Now get your brown desert jockey ass out of here." He reached under the bar and pulled out a revolver and placed it on the table. "Now. Get. Moving."

Zamir started to speak but Dani put a hand on his arm. "Let's go."

Outside Zamir turned to Dani. "You let him pull a gun on me. I've done nothing. You're a police officer, and you did not stop him?"

"Not today, Zamir. I couldn't do anything about it today."

"Not *today*?" Zamir turned away.

Dani turned away also, but for a different reason. She'd been off duty all day and she knew her department would still be on full alert. She walked to her car and drove to the Sheriff's office. The office was a hive of activity, and the Sheriff called to her as she walked in the door. "Dani, in my office now."

"Where the hell have you been?" he snapped.

"You knew where I was, I was on the mountain all day – I cleared it with you."

"Yeah, I knew where you were. And so do all the other guys in the department. I'm getting all kinds of flack that you're out with your Arab boyfriend on the day our country is under attack. It's a terrible look."

"He's not Arab, he's Iraqi. And he's a citizen, he's as American as you or me."

"Maybe. But right now, I can't have you here. Feelings are running too high. I'm giving you a couple of days off."

"What? I know you can't spare anyone right now with all the shit that's gone down. You're going to send me home because some redneck cowboys don't like people with brown skin?"

"I'm sorry. That's the way it is. Go home. Touch base with me tomorrow and we can see how it's going."

Dani was afraid she'd say something that would put her in deeper trouble than she was in already. She turned and walked out the door.

Dani's police radio squawked and pulled her back into the present. Putting the car into gear she headed back to the Sheriff's office along the same route she'd taken on that long ago day. She'd gone back to work three days after the triathlon, but she was shunned by the men in her department for the next couple of years. Luckily, due to the high housing cost to live in Jackson, there was huge turnover in the Sheriff's department and, five years later, no one was still around who remembered the episode. When she ran for Sheriff ten years later, she was afraid the past would be used against her, but it never surfaced. At least the police code of silence was good for something, she thought. Zamir left for Argentina the next day, informing her of his departure by way of a message on her answering machine, and she'd never spoken with him again. She'd felt badly about their parting for a long time. She second-guessed herself for not standing up to the bartender. Eventually she came to terms with September eleventh. It had been a terrifying day for the country, and extreme circumstances can bring out the best and worst in all of us, sometimes both within a few hours of each other.

When she walked into her office, Joanie looked up. "We just got a call from the highway patrol. There's a wreck in the Snake River Canyon. There may be someone trapped in the car."

"I'm on my way," Dani said, and walked back out the door.

FLOOR TIME

Hayden Smith watched as the family of four exited their Chrysler minivan with Missouri license plates and waddled toward the Jackson Hole Racquet Club condo. Naming the development just down the road from the Jackson Hole Ski Resort a Racquet Club wasn't completely fraudulent – there were half a dozen tennis courts in the 1970s-era neighborhood. The subdivision, a mix of local residents and short-term rentals owned by investors, hadn't been successful in attracting the tennis crowd, and the courts looked as if they hadn't seen a match in decades.

Hayden held out his hand. "You must be the Johnsons. I'm Hayden Smith, with Teton Real Estate. Nice to meet you."

Leonard Johnson, a man in his mid-forties with a third chin sprouting below his second and a generous belly threatening to escape his St. Louis Rams tee shirt, held out a fleshy paw. "Good to meet you. Thanks for meeting us on such short notice. We've been here a couple of weeks and my family just loves it. It's so beautiful, and the weather is perfect. When we left Missouri, it was ninety-five and humid."

Mrs. Johnson, who looked as if she could be Leonard's twin sister, added, "We just about died driving through Nebraska. The weather here is such a relief."

"Yes, the summers here are perfect," Hayden agreed. "So, you're looking for an investment property?"

"We had an idea to spend a few weeks here in the summer and maybe a week skiing every winter, and rent it out for income when we aren't here," said Leonard.

"Leonard and I are teachers," said Mrs. Johnson, and added, "We just love it out here, and it would be a good for the kids to spend some time in the summers outdoors, what with Teton National Park and Yellowstone just up the road."

A pre-teen boy and girl stood just behind the parents and appeared to be in the early stages of sharing their parents' physique. This did not strike him as a family that would be hiking the hundreds of miles of trails in the thousands of square miles of national park and national forest that comprises the wilderness area surrounding Jackson Hole.

"Yes," Hayden agreed. "I grew up in Ohio, and I came out here with my parents when I was just about their age. I came back to live here after I finished school. I can't imagine living anywhere else."

Hayden described the unit they were going to see – a second floor, two-bedroom unit with one of the bedrooms in a suite up another flight of stairs – and invited the family to take a look. Mrs. Johnson eyed the outside stairs that led to the front door. "Are there any units in this building at ground level?"

"There are," said Hayden, "but all the first-floor units are one bedroom." He wondered about the family's ability to explore the backcountry if they found the stairs to their unit a challenge. "The door's unlocked. Go ahead and take a look around and tell me what you think." He watched as the four huffed their way up the stairs and into the condo.

Hayden had discovered the Tetons in the summer of 1990 as a ten-year-old on a family vacation with his sister and parents. He'd been annoyed at leaving his friends for the summer, and at sitting in a car for hours on end in order to get to a destination he'd had no say about. He had spent most of the time with his face in his Nintendo Gameboy, looking up only periodically when his mother would yell at him about some scenic feature looming out the car window, and then would go right back to playing his video game. That had changed when they'd reached Teton National Park.

He'd resentfully raised his head and, when he looked up, he instantly recognized where he was. Dropping his

Gameboy on the floor, he pressed his face against the car window. "*Shane*! Mom, this is where the movie is from!"

Hayden had become obsessed with the 1953 Western ever since he'd seen it on TV and made his parents buy him a VHS copy for his birthday. In person, the Tetons looked just as they had in the movie, completely unreal. He'd watched the movie dozens of times and had come to believe the mountains were only a painted Hollywood backdrop. For the rest of the vacation in the Tetons, the Gameboy remained on the floor of the car, and he didn't pick it up again until the mountainscape had disappeared in the rear-view window.

By training, Hayden was an attorney, but he'd hated law school and never actually practiced. He'd enrolled in law school in the first place only because of a woman, following his college sweetheart to Ohio State Law. On graduation, she took a job in New York City. He would have moved there too, even though he hated big cities, but she told him it was better that he get on with his life, which did not include her. He took some time off then, before launching a search for a job somewhere far from the Big Apple, and went back to Jackson Hole. He never left.

When he'd arrived in town, he'd studied for and passed the Wyoming bar, but his heart still wasn't in it. The gorgeous luxury properties and the outrageous prices of real estate in the area, however, caught his eye, and he thought maybe he could make a career in it. It looked like a lot more fun than the law. Hayden was good looking, outgoing and friendly, and he figured those were the primary skills required in the profession, but his first two years in the business had been rough going. He knew no one, and he'd found out quickly that having a social network was critical to a successful real estate career. He made friends easily, but the other twenty-somethings he met in town weren't candidates to buy or sell real estate. They were mostly in town to hike, climb, or ski and could barely afford the ridiculous rents. Hayden himself shared a one-bedroom apartment with two other guys and bartended five days a week to supplement his income. He'd had the idea that he'd meet some more established people who might be interested in real estate by taking a bartending job at the Four Seasons, but he quickly realized that the wealthier customers at the upscale hotel wouldn't consider hiring a bartender as their real estate broker.

Hayden came to realize that his best source of leads was floor time and he'd signed up to take several shifts a week. The more established agents were happy to let him have the hours: floor time consisted of waiting, often alone, in the office for someone to call in about a real estate ad they'd seen in the local paper, or a for-sale sign they'd seen while driving through town. During the summer season, when the town was full of tourists, there were a lot of calls. Tourists commonly fell in love the first time they saw the Tetons, and many would entertain the fantasy of owning property here. Looking at real estate listings was just another featured entertainment attraction, and a free one at that. The serious buyer from a floor call is the real estate unicorn, and Hayden hadn't encountered one yet.

Leonard had called the office from a newspaper ad, and Hayden had caught the call on floor time. The family made their way down the stairs, and Hayden asked, "What do you think?"

Leonard and Mrs. Johnson paused to catch their breath, then Mrs. Johnson panted, "That unit was very outdated, and the appliances aren't stainless steel, and why is there no air conditioning in the unit?"

"Most of the units here don't have a/c. The evenings are cool and summer days are so mild that it isn't needed."

Leonard Johnson got right to the point. "What's the price?"

"This unit is five-hundred-ninety-five thousand. It's the lowest-priced two-bedroom in this subdivision."

The couple exchanged horrified glances. "That price is unbelievable. We had no idea prices here are so high. We were looking to spend around three-hundred-thousand…"

"Yes, the prices in this area are amongst the highest in the country. Only around three percent of Teton County is privately owned, and there are a lot of very rich people here with second homes that bid up the real estate prices. There are no two-bedroom units in the three-hundreds in Jackson. Now, if you'd want to drive across Teton pass to Driggs or Victor, or south to Alpine, there are condos in that price range. Those towns are around a forty-five-minute drive." Hayden didn't add that those locations across the pass were impractical for a winter vacation property because the roads were often closed by snow, and it would be difficult to rent them out to tourists in the summer.

"Well, thank you for showing us, Hayden," said Leonard. "But I think the prices here are a little out of our price range."

Before heading back to the office, Hayden was himself driving the forty-five minutes to Alpine to show a property. He'd taken a job at a bar in Jackson that catered to the working people of the community, and the few transactions he'd had over the last two years had come from people he'd met at that bar. He was showing a house in Alpine to an electrician who stopped in the bar after work several times a week before heading to his apartment there. He was showing him a tiny, two-bedroom, single-family home located in the town at the base of a dangerous, curvy road down the Snake River Canyon, affordable because of a difficult and dicey commute during the winter.

The next day Hayden was reading the Jackson Hole Daily News in his cubicle when a call was routed to him. "My employer is in town on holiday," the British-accented voice explained, "and would like to see some properties."

"OK, great," said Hayden. "Can I get some specifics? What kind of property does he have in mind, and what price range is he thinking of?"

"Well, he'd like to meet with you first to go through all of that. Could you come out and meet him this afternoon? He's staying at a house in Wilson. "

The house was twenty minutes from Jackson, two miles off Moose Wilson Road, up a long, narrow, gravel driveway. Constructed of logs and stone, it looked more like a lodge in the national park than a house. Obviously, the person who was renting it, as well as the person who owned it, were of substantial financial means.

A tall, thin man answered the door. "Good afternoon, Mr. Smith. My name is Robert. Thank you for coming. Please come with me." He led Hayden into a large room with a two-story, wood-beamed trussed ceiling. One wall of the room was glass, with full mountain vistas. The room's scale and its oversized furniture gave the feeling of a grand hotel in the Alps.

Hayden stood gazing at the window, when another British voice, this time in a lower, more sonorous range, greeted him. "Mr. Smith, thank you for coming."

Hayden turned and instantly recognized the man. He was shirtless – his hairless chest displaying every muscle and sinew – shoeless, and wearing ripped jeans. The man was shorter than Hayden might have expected, and his eyes were a piercing blue, deeper than the images of the man he'd seen many times before.

"It's my pleasure," said Hayden,

"I'm Winston Rathbone, call me Win."

"Yes, I recognize you. And please call me Hayden." Hayden laughed nervously at the absurdity of Win needing to introduce himself. Winston Rathbone was, at that moment in time, the most famous movie star in the world. His sci-fi action movie was the highest grossing movie of the year. Hayden knew this because he'd just read a magazine profile of Win while doing floor time in his office.

"Please, sit," said Winston, and he took a seat in an enormous leather chair and motioned to an identical chair next to him. Hayden thought his boyish face and compact body made him look like a child in the oversized furniture.

"I've decided to move to the United States permanently, and I need a place to live. It can't be LA. I hate it there, everything and everyone is so plastic. I love the American West. And, of course, this valley has such a rich cinematic history. Just look at that." He glanced to the window. "I've been entranced with this place ever since I saw the movie *Shane* as a little boy. I just love Alan Ladd – "

Hayden smiled. He told Win the story of his obsession with the movie and his trip to Wyoming as a ten-year-old. "I think it's probably the reason I was drawn back here after college."

Hayden still was a bit star struck, but Win asked him for more details of that trip, and what it had been like growing up in Ohio, and why he'd made the decision to give up the law. He had a way of putting Hayden at ease, not at all acting like a movie star, and Hayden started relating to him like any other client. "Of course, I'd be happy to show you some of the highlights of the valley while I'm helping you find your new home here. Now tell me, what kind of place are you looking for, and how much do you want to spend?" Hayden would normally ask what his price range was, which implied affordability, but he was talking to a man of great wealth and it was more about how much he wanted to spend.

"I don't have a price in mind. But what I'm looking for is land. A lot of land, with a view like this," he said, and nodded at the window again. "I'd rather not just buy vacant land, though. I'd like something with buildings on it. Maybe a ranch. Do you have any ranches for sale?"

Hayden had no idea if there were any ranches for sale. None of his clients had ever asked him about ranches before. "Oh, I'm sure we can find you a ranch. I'll put together some for us to look at. When would you like to meet again?"

"If you can find some properties to look at, I'm free tomorrow. But why don't we meet up for dinner tonight. Maybe you can show me around a bit. Take me to your favorite restaurant. I've heard there's some nice ones in town."

Hayden thought for a moment about fine dining in Jackson. There were a slew of four-star restaurants in town, but Hayden hadn't sampled many because of their prices. Then he thought of something else, but he hesitated to suggest –

"I'm sorry…" Win interrupted his thoughts. "What's wrong with me? I was being presumptuous. Perhaps you already have plans."

"No, not at all. I was just thinking of something. There are still some of the family homestead buildings from the original *Shane* set out near Kelly, about twenty minutes outside of town. Would you like to see them? We could stop on the way to dinner this evening. The light on the mountains is amazing right around sunset."

"I would love that!" said Win.

Back at the office, Hayden went through the listings for ranches. There were a lot of homes on ten to twenty acres that brokers called "ranches" in the listings, because wealthy second-homeowners liked to brag to their friends that they owned a ranch out west, but Hayden knew that Win wanted a real ranch. He was looking for properties over a hundred acres. He found only three for sale and called the listing brokers to set up appointments for the following day, and then stopped by their offices in town to pick up brochures on the properties. Now where should he and Win go for dinner? There were several Michelin-rated restaurants in town, and Hayden hadn't actually been to any of them. So he walked into the office of his managing broker and told her of his problem. When he mentioned that he'd picked up Winston Rathbone on a floor call, she was nearly speechless. She picked up her phone, "I know one of the owners of the Snake River Grill."

Hayden was concerned that they would be mobbed all evening by adoring fans, but when he picked Win up at his house that evening, he didn't recognize him. He was wearing a baseball cap, sunglasses, and a bushy jet-black beard, and when he spoke to Hayden it was with a southern accent. "I hope you don't mind," Win said, gesturing at his altered appearance. "I find it much easier to have a normal experience when I'm out in public."

"We probably won't meet anyone until we get into town. This location doesn't appear in the guidebooks and the only people who really know about it are locals, or true movie buffs. It's not easy to find unless you know what you're looking for."

"So, Hayden, you said you have an obsession with the movie. Do you mind if I test your obsession a little bit?"

"What do you have in mind?"

"How about a *Shane* trivia contest. The loser pays for dinner."

"Sure, but, ethically, I don't know if I'm permitted to take advantage of a client." He knew that he had enough space on his credit card for a pretty good dinner, but if Win went crazy with expensive wine, it could get embarrassing. Still, he was fairly sure he wouldn't lose.

They alternated trivia questions about *Shane*. Hayden knew the year the movie was made, the names of the co-stars nominated for Academy Awards, and Win laughed when Hayden answered that despite many nominations the only Oscar actually won was by the Tetons, for cinematography. Win knew that it was director George Stevens's only Western, that it was Jean Arthur's last movie role, and that it ranked 45 on the top 100 movies of all time by the American Film Institute. Hayden stumped Win by asking about the historical event that had inspired the movie – the bloody Johnson County range war in the late 1800s in Wyoming between homesteaders and cattlemen.

"Congratulations, Hayden. I'm very impressed. I hope you'll order an outrageously priced bottle of wine with dinner, because I was planning on it."

The dilapidated buildings of the *Shane* homestead were hidden behind a thick growth of cottonwoods off a gravel road east of the mountain range. Bushwhacking through the cottonwoods, and then a grove of aspens for a hundred yards or so, they came on a clearing and some log structures, overgrown with weeds and grasses. Win stopped and surveyed the site. It had obviously been chosen because of its full view of the Tetons, still unobstructed more than fifty years later due to its location on protected land adjacent to the national park. Win walked quietly around the small cabin, and then lowered his head to walk inside. The walls and roof of the cabin sagged dangerously, but the kitchen window still framed the perfect view of the Grand Teton that Jean Arthur and moviegoers would see as she washed dishes. Win smiled, "That's it. That's the view that hooked me."

"Me too," whispered Hayden.

Win walked around the set for a few more minutes, and then they got into Hayden's car and stared at the Teton Range. The sun was setting behind the mountains in the golden hour, and they sat quietly together, absorbing the scene of the iconic Western, a half-century later.

On the way back into town, Win spoke first. "That was amazing. I can't thank you enough. You know, I've always wanted to make a Western. I hope I can find the right script."

"Some say the movie you're in right now is just an outer-space Western."

Win laughed. "Some do say that, but you and I know that's just intellectual bullshit."

At the Snake River Grill, Win ordered an outrageously expensive bottle of wine, and they dined on locally-sourced dishes including elk and trout and enjoyed a delicious wild huckleberry tart for dessert.

They chatted through dinner, and Win seemed fascinated that Hayden had given up a law career and headed west. "Hayden, you embody the typical American spirit, the restlessness and desire to just pick up and head west. Just like the pioneers of the eighteen-hundreds."

Hayden was amused by Win's tendency to speak in hyperbole but put it down to Win's view of life as melodrama. Probably it was part of what made him such a great actor.

After dinner, Hayden took his new friend to a dive bar he liked, with music and dancing, and as they sat at the bar drinking, one of Hayden's old friends came up to him. "Hey, dude what's up? I thought you were working tonight at the Cellar, but when I went there, they told me you don't work there anymore. What happened?"

Hayden had called in sick to go out with Win, and the owner had fired him on the spot. Summer was the busiest season in Jackson, and it was unacceptable to call in sick unless you were completely incapacitated. "Oh, I had to quit that job. I'm too busy with my real estate business lately." Hayden didn't want the Hollywood star to know that he had to moonlight just to make ends meet. His friend glanced at the bearded man next to Hayden but gave no sign of recognition.

"That's cool. By the way, everybody's saying that Winston Rathbone's in town. Have you seen him?"

Hayden smiled. "No, but I'll keep my eye out."

Hayden was quiet after his friend left, and Win said. "Look, Hayden, I want you to be authentic with me. I know you're young and you're trying to get started in the business. There's no shame in bartending while you're trying to make it. I waited tables for five years in London and shared a flat with four other blokes before I got a break. I'd rather have you helping me with this than some old codger."

"Thanks, Win. I appreciate that." Hayden took a long swallow of his Wyoming Whiskey and changed the subject, describing the three ranches they would be seeing the next day. On the way home, they stopped by Hayden's office, and Hayden gave him the thick glossy brochures with pictures and detailed information on each of the properties. After dropping Win at his house, Hayden drove back to his apartment in town and climbed in his single bunk in the bedroom he shared with two other guys. The thought of a huge payday kept running through his mind and was nearly enough to drown out the cacophony of his snoring roommates.

The three listing agents who met Hayden and Win for the showings, one at each of the properties, were all women in their early fifties. Hayden knew the women's names but had never met any them. He remembered what a surprise it had been when he'd discovered the dominance of women in real estate, but, after he'd thought about it, he'd realized that real estate was one of the few professions without a glass ceiling. Success was based solely on merit, and women realtors outdid men in most parts of the country in income and production. It was also a profession in which social skills were as important as competitive drive, and Hayden thought that combination was more balanced in women than in men.

Win took no measures to disguise his identity on their second day together, and Hayden introduced him to the agents by his real name. The women showed no indication of being intimidated by his celebrity, but all of them asked if he was planning on living in Wyoming full-time versus LA, a subtle acknowledgment of his fame without fawning over it. Hayden wondered how long it would take him to become immune to the anxiety of dealing with clients of immense wealth and status.

Hayden could tell that Win was not impressed with the first two properties. Although they had mountain views, the views from the residences did not match those of the property he was renting. Win became more animated when they toured the third property, by far the largest of the three, with the best views of the Tetons and, additionally, with direct access to the Snake River. The property had a seven-thousand square foot main residence, a three-thousand square foot guest house, and a barn that had once housed equipment on what had been, for decades, a working ranch but was now remodeled into a structure that could be used for entertaining large parties. The agent explained that this ranch was owned by a trust controlled by the heirs of one of the richest industrialists of the last century, and the family just didn't use the property anymore. It was listed at sixty-million dollars, which would make it potentially the largest private property sale in Teton County in the last decade.

"I'm not interested at all in the first two places," Win said when they were back at his rental home, "but

I am very interested in the third. It's exactly what I'm looking for. What do you think I should offer for it?"

Hayden had done an analysis of comparables early that morning at his office and brought out his spreadsheets. There wasn't a direct comp based on the scale of this property, so he based his value on recent sales of ranches that were somewhat smaller than the subject property but with similar locations and buildings, adjusting for size. "I really don't think it's priced extravagantly, based on these comps. I'd suggest we test their flexibility and offer fifty and see what they say."

Win thought for a moment. "That sounds good. Put together a contract and we can fax that to my attorney to take a look. Would you be able to do that here? We have a computer and a fax machine in the office."

Hayden was surprised that this was moving so fast, but Win led him from the great room to a large room off the main hallway. The home office seemed like the rest of the house, almost too large for its purpose – the desk and credenza sitting like lonely islands at the end of the room. Hayden prepared the offer and faxed it to Win's attorney. Then Win spoke with his attorney by phone and, within an hour, the attorney sent back some changes. Hayden made the changes and faxed the contract to the listing agent. "Now we wait," he said.

"When do you think we'll get a response?"

"Hard to say, but there are multiple family members involved in this decision, so it may be awhile. I'll keep in contact with the listing agent."

Hayden left Win and spent the night tossing and turning. This commission could potentially be over half a million dollars, and that amount of money would change his life. The next morning, he got a call from the listing agent. "I have some bad news. The family has rejected your offer, and they're choosing not to counter."

"What's wrong? Were they insulted that the offer was too low? It was just a starting point," said Hayden.

"It's not the price, although they do think it's way too low. They said they don't want to sell it to Winston Rathbone. They said to tell him it's because of Patricia Holland."

Hayden drove out to Win's residence to deliver the bad news in person. "What's the significance of Patricia Holland?"

Win sighed. "I guess I'm not totally surprised this came up. She was the wife of one of the family members. I had an affair with her a long time ago. I was young and full of myself, and I'd just achieved some fame. She was star struck. It meant nothing to me, but they divorced because of it."

Win thought for a moment. "Offer them sixty-two and see if money can solve this."

Hayden made the call to the other broker, and Robert served them lunch, though Hayden had trouble eating. He was nauseous at the thought of the deal falling apart. Just as lunch was concluded, the broker called back. "I understand," Hayden said.

Hayden looked at Win, trying to smile. Trying not to grimace. "The family absolutely will not sell the property to you at any price. It's not about the money."

Win shrugged. "The penalties of sin. We never know when or how we have to pay for them do we?"

Driving back to town, Hayden was numb. He'd found the unicorn, but it had escaped, taking his only dependable source of income, his bartending job, with it. He went back to his office, signed in, and fielded calls from tourists the rest of the day.

The next morning, he awoke at three AM with an idea, and at nine called the only professional friend he had in town. Hayden had met Jake Simpson, a local about Hayden's age who was VP of lending at the largest local bank in town, at a Chamber of Commerce networking event, and they'd hit it off. Jake had advanced quickly at the bank, perhaps because its president and controlling shareholder was his father, and he and Hayden had become fast friends. Over lunch that afternoon, Hayden outlined his problem, and his potential solution.

"Hayden," Jake exclaimed, "that's brilliant. Let me talk to my dad. He knows a lot of people, and there's a chance this could work."

Hayden didn't hear back from his friend for a week – during which Win had been called back to the Coast to dub some scenes in his latest film – but finally Jake called. "Can you take a meeting at our office at noon?"

"Of course," said Hayden.

"And wear a suit."

Jake Simpson, Ralph Simpson, the bank President, and a third man Hayden had never met, were at the meeting. The third man was introduced as Miller Rourke, the founder of a large investment fund.

"Hayden and Jake, I want to thank you both for bringing this opportunity to us. I've been discussing this with Miller. He and I went to business school together a life time ago, and he's willing to come in and help us with this. The purpose of this meeting it to outline the solution and a plan of action. Miller is willing to act as a proxy for the real buyer in this transaction, assuming we can work out a deal for the purchase of the ranch. The funds for the purchase will be put up by our bank, and the deed will be transferred twenty-four hours after closing to Mr. Rathbone. Hayden, you will act as the broker for Miller, and negotiate the best deal you can. However, we all need to be compensated appropriately for this transaction. Miller will agree to transfer the deed to Mr. Rathbone for his purchase price plus four million dollars. Of the four million in profit, our bank will take two million of that for financing the purchase, Miller will take one million for acting as the proxy. Hayden, you will be paid legal consulting fee for this transaction of one million dollars. Does that sound fair to everyone?"

Hayden was stunned. He really just wanted to be able to get his commission on the deal, but he managed to squeak out, "Yes. I think that's fair."

"What we need for you to do is to get Mr. Rathbone to agree to this. If he does, we can work out the details with his attorney. We'll also need Mr. Rathbone to deposit funds in our bank to guarantee performance on the purchase from Miller. Miller, you don't want to own a ranch in Jackson, right?"

Miller laughed. "That's right, Ralph. I love Jackson Hole, but I don't want to be holding a sixty-million-dollar illiquid asset."

Hayden called Robert, and it took two weeks for Win to get back to him. It felt like the longest two weeks of his life – Hayden was sure Win must have changed his mind.

"Sorry I couldn't get back to you sooner," said Win. "I'm on location in Romania right now. So, you have a way I can buy the ranch?"

Hayden explained the plan and Win seemed agreeable. "So how much is this going to cost me?"

"Remember you were willing to pay sixty-two million when they turned you down. I'm pretty sure we can get it for less than that even with the four million bonus, provided they don't have any other offers."

"I'll call my attorney right now and give him the go ahead for a max all-in price of no more than sixty-two.

You can deal directly with him after that; he has complete power of attorney to act for me."

Three days later Win's attorney approved the plan, and Hayden put in an offer on the property on behalf of Miller Rourke. They negotiated a price of fifty-five and a half million and, with the four million in deal fees, the total cash out to Win would be fifty-nine and a half million. Win called Hayden to thank him when the deal closed forty-five days later, but he was so busy filming he didn't get a chance to visit his new ranch until six months later.

On a snowy winter afternoon, Hayden's assistant walked into his office with a familiar face trailing behind her. "This man says he needs to see you."

When Hayden saw Win, he stood, and Win put him in a bear hug. "I just stopped by to thank you for all your help. I went to your old office and they told me you don't work there anymore. I see you've come up in the world. I like the sign out front – Hayden Smith Properties. Well, well, well – "

"No, I should be thanking you. You had the faith that I could pull it off – "

Win demurred. "That deal was dead. I have to tell you I was really depressed when I went back to LA. You knew how much I wanted that place, and you didn't give up. You brought it back to life. I have a feeling you're going to do very well for yourself in this business. Can you come out to the ranch for dinner tonight? I'm entertaining a few guests from out of town, and I'd like them to meet you."

"Of course, I'd love to."

Years later, a new broker in Hayden's office complained about the mandatory floor time required of all new agents. "This is such a waste of time. All these damned tourists are just using us as tour guides. None of them are serious."

Hayden smiled. "Have a seat. Let me tell you a story."

THE WIFE

Lydia McGraw had many acquaintances but few friends. In fact, as she watched Carol Simpson pick at the chopped salad on her plate, she realized she really had only one friend. Lydia was a strategist, and many of her acquaintances – who believed they were, in fact, Lydia's friends – had been selected and wooed only because they provided her with some strategic advantage in creating the life that she had now. She had learned this life lesson from Carol in middle school.

Carol was the pretty, popular girl who had befriended Lydia when Lydia's scrawny frame, large nose, and gapped front teeth had led to humiliating sixth-grade bullying. When Carol brought her into her circle, Lydia learned that having the right friends could improve everything in her life. Carol's friendship wasn't altogether altruistic. Carol's physical beauty and social skills weren't accompanied by an equal quantity of intellect, and Lydia became Carol's personal tutor through junior high, high school, and the University of Wyoming. Their friendship began as a transactional relationship but grew into genuine affection over the decades. Carol was the only person in Lydia's life she felt she could truly trust, and that included her husband.

Carol swallowed a forkful of salad and looked up at Lydia. "He's having an affair. You say you haven't had sex in a couple of months, he's dieting, and he has a new wardrobe. So, who is it? Are there any attractive women on his staff?"

"No, there aren't," Lydia assured her. "I learned from your experience. I don't think there are any women on his staff who would be tempting to him." After Carol had caught her husband in an affair with his assistant, Lydia had gone on defense and taken over the task of interviewing all new hires for her own husband's staff. Although she insisted that half of his staff be female – she was ever tuned to the political optics – she made sure those who weren't overtly lesbian were, in her opinion, sufficiently unattractive so she was sure her husband wouldn't be tempted.

"How about lobbyists? You know that state senator from Cheyenne just got caught with a Sierra Club lobbyist. You'd think he'd be smarter than that. A Wyoming Republican doesn't come out in favor of stopping a gas pipeline because of some pronghorn migration unless there's some hanky-panky somewhere."

"I keep a copy of his calendar, and I've been watching him pretty closely. In my heart, I don't think he's having an affair. Tom has never had a high sex drive, but we've never gone this long before either. Maybe it's male menopause."

"Maybe." Carol looked skeptical. "Look Lydia, Tom is the best-looking guy in the United States Senate. He's been getting a lot of press lately and, frankly he's been saying some things that people in the party think are kind of crazy. Maybe he's having a mid-life crisis or something. I've been around long enough to know that when a man starts acting different at his age, it usually means there's another woman somewhere."

"We're going to be staying in town through the weekend, after the conference is over. So maybe I'll try to heat things up, and if he's not interested, then we'll need to have a talk."

Lydia and Carol were attending the annual banking conference in Jackson Hole, where Senator McGraw was the keynote speaker. The McGraws had a ranch near Cheyenne but, since Tom had been elected to Senate, they'd been spending more and more time in DC, and Lydia and Carol had been spending less time together. Carol's husband was the CEO of the largest privately-owned bank in Wyoming, based in Jackson Hole, and this annual conference had become a way for the two friends to catch up. She was grateful that Carol was here. She'd always listened to Lydia's problems without judgment and had taught her that sometimes you had to put yourself before your spouse.

After lunch with Carol, Lydia headed down to the meeting rooms. She was leading a seminar – along with the business education teacher-of-the-year in Wyoming, and a bank officer from one of the Big Four national banks – promoting a program for community banks to sponsor high-school finance education. This was Lydia's pet cause – she'd seen the damage done to so many families' finances across the country as a result of easy access to high-interest-rate credit cards that consumers were inundated with as soon as they graduated from high school.

After the seminar, she had a facial and massage scheduled at the hotel spa, and time to think more about her problem with her husband. They'd been college sweethearts, though Lydia had been shocked when Tom had shown interest in her. Her previous boyfriends had been nerds, and Tom was the opposite of that – outgoing, popular, and handsome. He was so strikingly good looking in college, in fact, he was almost pretty. As he'd gotten older, his boyish good looks had hardened a bit, and now he was as ruggedly handsome as a model in a magazine ad for camping equipment.

After their junior year, when he'd nearly failed every one of his classes, she'd broken up with him and gone out on a few dates with a computer engineering major. One night after she'd come home from a date, Tom had shown up at her sorority house and begged her for one last chance. She'd given him that chance, on the condition that she take over management of his life – monitoring his class attendance, his study habits, and severely restricting his partying. To her surprise he'd accepted and even thrived under her structure. After college, Lydia's father, the CEO of an energy conglomerate, had gotten Tom an internship at the office of the U.S. Senator from Wyoming and that experience, along with her father's contacts, eventually led to his election to the Wyoming legislature, and four years ago to the U.S. Senate. Lately, he'd grown more independent of her influence and distant from her. She wasn't sure what was going on, but she knew she needed to get to the bottom of it.

Her husband was tied up all day in meetings, and he'd already left to prepare his keynote address when Lydia got back to their suite to get ready for the evening. She met him backstage, where he was going over his speech with his friend and the organizer of the conference, Charles Kidwell, and a pretty dark-haired woman who Lydia did not recognize.

Tom stood and embraced Lydia. "I'm sorry we missed each other earlier, but I hope to cut out as soon as my speech is over and meet you upstairs. Darling, you know Charles, and this is Ana Perez. She's a friend of Charles and has been helping me with my speech."

Lydia looked Ana over. She was an attractive, thirty-something Hispanic woman.

Ana held out her hand, "So glad to meet the woman behind the man, Mrs. McGraw. I've heard a lot about you."

"Please call me Lydia. Have you been working with Senator McGraw long? I didn't know he'd hired a speech writer. He's always written his own speeches before."

Ana smiled, showing a mouthful of perfect, sparkling teeth, "Charles and I are old friends, and he brought me in a few weeks ago to help with messaging."

Tom interrupted. "Charles looked at my speech and thought it needed more punch and suggested that maybe a professional could help. We're actually making a few last-minute changes now, so I'll see you in our suite afterwards, OK?"

Lydia managed a smile before she walked away. Tom hadn't told her he was adding to his staff, and he'd never made hiring decisions in the past without running it by her. He'd certainly never *dismissed* her before. She took her seat in the front row next to her friend Carol and Carol's husband. Carol whispered, "Tom stopped by to say hello a few minutes ago. He was with a very cute lady. Is she new?"

Lydia gritted her teeth. "She's his new speech writer. I met her for the first time just now."

Tom had never before wanted professional help with his speeches. He'd always said he didn't want to be a "manufactured candidate". Lydia had been his chief editor, reviewing his drafts and making suggestions that Tom would agree with more often than not. Then Tom had met Charles Kidwell at a conference in Chicago a couple of years ago, and they'd become very close.

Lydia understood that Charles's financial and economic expertise had elevated Tom's mastery of those issues, but it seemed now that Charles was taking a much larger role. Hiring a speechwriter? Could the beautiful young woman be the wedge that had distanced the two of them?

A few minutes later Charles Kidwell, who was hosting the conference, introduced Senator McGraw to the audience. Charles was a Chicago banker who'd recently expanded his Midwest bank holdings by purchasing a group of troubled banks in Colorado, Wyoming, Idaho, Utah, and Montana. With his leadership, this banking conference was now the largest west of the Mississippi, and several hundred of the most influential bankers in the western United States filled the room. As Lydia listened to her husband's speech, she was shocked at what she heard. Someone had punched up his message, all right. He was telling the bankers in the room that they needed to clean up their act, and Lydia could tell the message wasn't going over very well.

"You all caught a break after the mortgage meltdown of 2008. The government bailed you out, and then a few reforms were proposed, and then every banker in the country whined and wailed about government regulation. The watered-down rules that were passed did nothing to dampen your profits, and now you're making more money than ever. And is our country any safer from financial catastrophe? I would argue that it is not. The same four banks are still too big to fail today. And many of your practices are still predatory and speculative. One of the banks represented in this room has just admitted to creating thousands of fraudulent bank accounts in the names of their customers. Many of you are enticing consumers to take out credit-card debt at rates that would embarrass local loan sharks. A reckoning is coming, ladies and gentlemen. And it would behoove you to get out ahead of it."

As Senator McGraw kept on going, people started walking out of the room. At the end of his speech, the room was silent.

Carol whispered to Lydia, "What the hell is he doing?"

Lydia shrugged and stared straight ahead, afraid to make eye contact with Carol's husband.

A crowd gathered around Tom at the dais at the end of his speech, and Lydia could see he was going to be engaged for a while, so she returned to her room. She changed into casual clothes and stood in front of the mirror. She knew she wasn't particularly good looking, but she made the best of what she had – great skin, her makeup was always done perfectly, and she still weighed the same as she had in college. Her breasts were so small she didn't like wearing a bathing suit, but she thought her shapely legs made up for it. What was wrong with Tom? What was he trying to accomplish with a speech like that? He'd been a traditional conservative Republican when he'd been elected, but over the last year he'd been espousing different ideas, and it correlated in some way with his lack of interest in sex with her, she was sure of this.

She curled up on the couch, picked up the novel she'd been reading, but found herself unable to concentrate on the words, obsessed with thoughts of what was going on with her husband. She felt a migraine coming on and took a pain killer. She woke much later, groggy, when she felt someone tugging at her arm. "What time is it?'

"It's late. A bunch of the bankers were not happy with what I had to say tonight, and I had some drinks with them so they could tell me how I was wrong. I texted you earlier."

"Sorry," she said, brushing her rumpled hair out of her face with both hands, making a snap decision that she would rather hear the worst from Tom than go on suffering a headache every time she thought about him. "We need to talk. What's going on with us? What's going on with you? You haven't been yourself, and where is all this anti-business stuff coming from?"

"I know things must seem a bit strange to you. Can we talk about this in the morning? I'm exhausted."

Lydia laid awake for hours, angry and confused at the change in him. She glared at him, laying there, snoring loudly as if he hadn't a care in the world. She elbowed him hard and the snoring stopped as he turned on his side. She ran through all the possibilities in her head, but nothing really made sense. It *had* to be that woman.

When she awoke early, as she always did, Tom was still asleep. She got up and took a shower, put on makeup and a nightgown she'd bought especially for this trip, brewed Tom a cup of coffee and took it to the bedroom, sitting on the edge of the bed next to him. She touched his face, and he awoke.

"Good morning. How do you feel?"

"I'm fine. I really only had a couple of beers, if that's what you think." He sat up and took the coffee from her. "You're looking sexy this morning. What's the occasion?"

"Well… we haven't for a while, and I thought –"

"You thought what?" Tom smiled and put his coffee down. "That maybe I'd like to make love to my beautiful wife?" He took her in his arms.

Afterward, he kissed her gently. "That was nice."

"*Nice?* That's it? Just nice? After I spent the last hour trying to make myself desirable for you. Why don't you want me anymore, Tom?" Her voice was hoarse with hurt and anger, but she would not let him see her cry.

"That's not true. I do want you. Didn't I show you just now?"

"This is the first time we've made love in three months. And you said it was… *nice* …and you have all these… new ideas. You're making a lot of enemies, you know? The hands that feed you…"

Tom was alarmed at this side of Lydia. He couldn't remember the last time they'd had a fight. He took a sip of the coffee, now cold and bitter in his mouth.

"You're right. I do have a lot of new ideas. The world is changing, and our party hasn't. I haven't accomplished anything since I've been in the Senate, and I don't want my service to be for nothing. I'm saying what I really think for the first time in my life. Ever since I got into politics, somebody else has been telling me what to think. Your father, the party leaders, all the people that fund my campaigns. And, yes, even you. I'm tired of living like that."

"And you're tired of everything, including me. I get it. Your new speechwriter, she's beautiful," Lydia shouted. She knew she was losing control, and the fact that Tom was making her lose control made her even angrier.

Tom hadn't seen this side of her since she'd broken up with him back in college. "I'm not having an affair with my speechwriter," he sputtered. "It's just as I said – Charles brought her in to help out. And, no, I'm definitely not tired of you. If not for you, I'd be working in a gas field somewhere in Casper."

Lydia didn't speak. She went into the bathroom and washed her face. When she came out, she'd calmed herself and spoke softly to Tom. "What do you say we order some breakfast?"

They had room service in the suite, and Tom had a meeting in town with the owner of a wind farm later that morning. "I'll be back before lunch. What do you say we pack a picnic and drive out to Jenny Lake? It's going to be a beautiful day."

"That sounds lovely," Lydia said, but after Tom left for his meeting, she couldn't get the conversation they'd had out of her head. It did sound to her as if Tom was going through some kind of mid-life crisis. She loved being a senator's wife, it was more than she'd ever thought possible when she decided to marry the reformed frat boy twenty years ago. Now he was on the verge of throwing it all away. She picked up her phone and called Charles Kidwell's room. "Charles, this is Lydia McGraw. We need to talk."

"Good morning, Lydia. I think we definitely need to talk, but probably without Tom around."

"Tom's in town for a meeting for a couple of hours. Can you come up to our suite?"

Lydia had met Charles several times, and they'd exchanged small talk and pleasantries. What she knew about him was only what Tom had shared with her. Now she looked at him carefully as he sat in the chair in front of her. He was about the same age as she and her husband, a tall, thin man, with a long face, a prominent nose, and thinning dark hair. She suddenly realized that he looked very much like a male version of herself, and she wasn't sure how she felt about that.

"I'm going to be very blunt with you, Charles. Tom hasn't been the same for the last year or so. He has all these crazy ideas. That speech last night was a disaster.

And I think he's ruining his political prospects. I think you have something to do with this."

Charles smiled nervously. He'd purposely tried to stay clear of Lydia. He'd had only superficial conversations with her in the past, and he knew from conversations with Tom how much influence she had over him, so he'd been treading lightly for some time. She was frowning at him now, actually drumming her fingers on the table beside her.

"Lydia, I've noticed the same changes in Tom since we met. But it's not me, I assure you. About a year ago, Tom started to talk about his evolving political views. He said he felt he'd been forced into some kind of political orthodoxy. I told him that he had a very good career and could work within his party for some changes, but if he went public with all of his disagreements with his party, he would be ostracized."

"Well, he clearly took *that* bit of advice to heart." Her sardonic wit was evident.

"Lydia, he said he didn't care. He was done living a life that wasn't his own. I thought a long time about it and, frankly, I'm in awe of his courage in doing this. Politically, mostly, I agree with you, but there's a way that this could work out for him. It's risky, but — That's what I wanted to talk with you about." Charles paused. This conversation was not going as he expected, but he moved forward anyway. "Do you like being a senator's wife?"

"It's more than I ever thought could happen to me."

"What would you think of being First Lady?"

She didn't say anything for a moment, and then a low-pitched guffaw seemed to emerge from deep within her. Charles had never seen her laugh before, but the deep tone was so shocking that Charles had to smile.

"You're not serious." She tilted her head and looked at him quizzically.

"I am. You said Tom's been talking about all these crazy things. Haven't you noticed he's getting a lot of national attention on CNN and all the political shows now? That wasn't happening a year ago. He's the most sought-after Republican senator now on all the political talk shows, by both sides of the spectrum. He hasn't been talking just to the people of Wyoming. He's been talking to the entire country. I commissioned a private poll, and he's the most popular Republican Senator with independent voters. He has a chance of staking a claim in the party. Of transforming the party. I think he's got a real shot in the next election. The nomination is likely going to be wide open."

Tom had never revealed any political ambitions beyond being a United States Senator, and even that had been her idea. "And what happens if he makes a fool of himself? You know... Wyoming is a very conservative state, and some of his ideas – Well. He could lose his Senate seat."

"He could, yes. But Western voters are a very independent breed. Not long ago, Wyoming had a Demo-

cratic governor, and Montana has a Democratic Senator now. Voters see Tom as honest, straight-talking, and
independent. Plus, he scores off the charts in likeability."

Lydia was silent for a minute. "I don't know what to say."

"I've spent a lot of time with him over the last year.
I think his mind is made up to share his views with the
world. You saw what he did last night. Those weren't my
ideas, and they weren't Ana's. They were Tom's. We can
get on the bus with him, or we can let him drive it alone.
And, make no mistake, Tom's the one in the driver's seat.
If he's going to drive it off a mountainside, I want to be
with him. The question is, do you?"

It was hard for her to process the enormity of what
Charles was telling her in the moment. All she could
think was that her world was about to change, one way
or the other. "What if I can't support this?"

"I'm pretty sure he can't win the nomination without you. You're the poised, calm, stable offset to him. It
plays very well. He's not going anywhere without you."

Lydia nodded. "I'm going to have to give this a lot
of thought. But there's another thing. I need you to be
honest with me. Is Tom having an affair with Ana?"

Charles wasn't surprised at the question. When
Lydia had said she felt he was the cause of the change
in Tom, he'd been alarmed. A question about Ana he'd
been ready for.

"Definitely not," he said, and then repeated for
emphasis, "I'm sure he is not. She's here only to help with

speech-writing and to develop a strategy for his national message. They are not involved. In fact, Ana likes girls."

"It's important that you're honest with me. If I agree to this, and find out later he's sleeping with another woman, I will leave him, middle of a campaign or not."

"I swear. He's not seeing another woman."

When Tom returned, he and Lydia stopped by a deli on the way out of town and picked up some food for their picnic. Tom rented a boat at Jenny Lake, and they spent the afternoon in the calm alpine lake in the shadow of the Teton Range. They didn't talk politics, or about the conference, and Lydia didn't mention the meeting with Charles. They simply dropped anchor in the middle of the lake and shared wine and cheese and bread. It was a beautiful afternoon together, but when Tom kissed her, she wondered if he was thinking of Ana. Was Charles was just covering for his friend?

Lydia thought about her conversation with Charles all week, and she read a book profiling each of the president's wives. She imagined what it would be like as First Lady, what Tom might do if she told Charles she wasn't interested.

Lydia was supposed to fly to DC on Friday morning, but she changed it to a flight Thursday evening instead. She wanted Carol's take on her husband's behavior and the conversation with Charles. They had dinner at Carol's favorite restaurant. It was as they were finishing their appetizers that, in the corner of the crowded dining room, Lydia saw her husband in a booth. Sitting next to him, on the same side of the booth, was Ana Perez. Lydia watched as Ana reached up and, with her napkin, laughed as she brushed a crumb from Tom's face.

"I'm sorry, Carol, I have a terrible migraine. I'm going to have to just go home and go to bed. Please, forgive me." She fled before she could be spotted by Tom and Ana.

When Lydia got home, she poured herself a tall gin and tonic over ice and picked up the phone to call her friend. She'd been too upset about what she'd seen at the restaurant to have the conversation there, but even now she hung up the phone before Carol could answer. At that moment she knew Carol would support her in whatever she decided, but she also knew that Carol couldn't help her with the actual decision. Lydia's path forward needed to be about not what her friend would do, or what was best for her husband. It had to be about what was best for her.

She took a deep breath, picked up the phone, and dialed a different number. "Hello, Charles, it's Lydia. I've made up my mind. Go ahead, full speed. Make me First Lady."

She fell back in her chair and realized her migraine was starting to fade. Taking a deep swig from her glass, she savored the combination of the bitter tonic with the ice-cold herbal gin. Picking up her book from the table, she turned to the page profiling the First Lady of the forty-second President.

SELF-MADE MAN

Daryl Fay floated to the surface of his sedation fog into the blinding light of the hospital ward. The halogen lamp stabbing his eyes wasn't the warm glow described in the near-death experiences he'd read about in the books from the prison library – not that he'd been expecting a heavenly family reunion with his parents. If they'd been there, he would have known he'd been sent to that other place. Daryl didn't believe in the religious fairy tales his father had tried to beat into him; he'd really just been looking forward to a nice, long, black void free of pain. He looked down at his aching arms strapped to the bed, wrapped in gauze stained with his dried blood. The plastic knife he'd manage to smuggle from the prison cafeteria, and then spent hours sharpening on a rough edge on the concrete floor of his cell, hadn't done the trick. Like everything else in the twenty-two years of his life, he'd managed to fuck this up, too.

The prison chaplain – an amiable, overstuffed Episcopal priest – entered the room and walked to his bedside. Daryl had endured a one-on-one session with Father Forster as part of his "intake orientation" three weeks ago, and had attended one of the priest's Sunday services, too, not because he had any religious inclination, but as part of his short-lived plan to try to ingratiate himself with as many parole influencers as possible.

"I'm glad to see you're awake. How are you doing?" Father asked.

Daryl focused on the beads of sweat on the priest's wide forehead. In his groggy state, he thought the droplets looked like condensation on a can of cold beer. He could use a cold one right about now. In his imagination, the man of God's sweating each time he'd seen him was because he knew in his heart that he really was a man of Con, and he felt guilty about dispensing his continuous line of biblical bullshit.

"Not so good, Father." Daryl nodded toward his left arm. "I was trying to carve a face of the Virgin Mary into my arm… and I guess I went a little too deep."

Father Forster ignored the sacrilege. "I know you're hurting, Daryl. It's common for younger inmates to have issues with depression when they're first incarcerated. I want you to know that I'm here for you. And Jesus is here for you, too."

"Oh, yeah," Daryl slurred. "Sweet baby Jesus. Can you ask him where he was when my dad was beating the shit out of me when I was eight years old?"

Daryl's botched suicide attempt resulted in five days in the mental ward, a psych evaluation, medication, and mandatory attendance at a daily prison therapy group. He wasn't a novice to the process. He'd been diagnosed with bipolar disorder and depression at fourteen, when he stole a car and headed for California under the illusion that Shia LaBeouf had been talking to him from the screen of a *Transformers* movie. He didn't get far. Caught shoplifting at a truck stop off of I-80, he'd spent the rest of his teens at a home for delinquent youth. When he was released on his eighteenth birthday, he moved to Alpine, a small community south of Jackson Hole, and commuted there to his job as a bellman at the Four Seasons, supplementing his income by supplying a little weed to the tourists. It wasn't the tourists that got him in trouble. He was busted in Alpine for selling to some loose-lipped high-school kids and felt lucky his public defender was able to plead out the charge, but the deal still got him nine months' prison time. He'd been off his meds for several months before his arrest, and after three weeks in prison, he'd bottomed out.

The prison doctor had started him back on anti-depressants, but when Daryl told the story of his salvation, as he often did now to strangers as part of his current business, he said there were two additional things that changed his life. The first was his discovery in the prison library. After his discharge from the hospital, he'd been assigned a job in the library and spent his free time devouring their entire self-help collection. He'd always liked to read, never the books assigned to him in school, but there was something about the hodgepodge collection of donated books in the prison that appealed to him. He discovered a thirty-year-old paperback titled, *Inventing Yourself* by Andrew Adler. Adler's theory had three simple parts that seemed to dovetail perfectly with Daryl's specific neuroses. First principle: all humans have unlimited potential that is artificially constrained by their parents, institutions, society, and themselves. Second: it is up to each individual to create for themselves a life of their own design and reject the one they are assigned to by the accident of the circumstances to which they are born. Finally: no one gets rich by working for someone else, and the only path to true freedom, happiness, and wealth is through entrepreneurship. The masses are ignorant, Adler advised, because even those in the lowest paying jobs are already creating wealth every single day – for the wealthy entrepreneurs who exploit their labor. Like many before him, Daryl had found the religious experience he'd never had in Sunday school through this version of the American Dream. The photo on the back cover portrayed a very young man. Daryl searched for more publications by Adler in the library's limited inventory, but without success.

After his release from prison, Daryl went back to Alpine and took a job bartending six nights a week and working days at the front desk at the motel next door.

He lived a monastic life in his camper on a site next to the Grey's river, saving every penny of his wages for the right entrepreneurial opportunity. That came the afternoon he took himself to the Jackson Hole library, the nearest decent library to Alpine, and googled "Andrew Adler entrepreneur". He discovered that Andrew had his own web site, and had apparently found the right entrepreneurial opportunity for himself; in his generosity, he'd decided to share it with the entire world. On the site was an announcement for a weekend seminar in Salt Lake City, and Daryl arranged to have that weekend off by working thirty days straight at his two jobs.

The second event that changed his life occurred the evening he came to his bartending job and discovered a work crew putting the final touches on a new flashing neon sign outside of the building. The owner gathered the employees together and explained the bar was being renamed "The Grandest Tetons," and the new business model would be: "Food, Dancers, Cocktails, Dancers, Lodging, Dancers." The closing time would now be extended to 2 AM, and the owner promised that the additional business would likely double his tip income. Later that afternoon a half-dozen dancers arrived, hired in from an establishment in Idaho Falls that had been shut down by religious activists. The buddies Daryl ran with after the juvie home had loved strip clubs. He'd watched them blow their paychecks on watered-down drinks and lap dances, but he'd never really found the concept that appealing. He'd seen the blank stares of the women as they took off their clothes for his drunken friends, and he didn't find it sexy. If a woman was going to take her clothes off for him, he wanted it to be a romantic rather than a monetary exchange. That being said, he made no judgments regarding anyone's choice of occupation, and although he found many of the dancers very attractive, he couldn't imagine being in a relationship with them. That is, until he laid eyes on Amber Gathers.

The moment Amber walked in the door, he found himself mesmerized by her. It wasn't just that she was young, blonde, and pretty. What hypnotized Daryl was her large blue eyes and her angelic look of innocence. Her demeanor wasn't just shy, it was timid, and at first Daryl thought she didn't like him. As the days went by, he observed her carefully and could see that she was cautious and reserved in her interactions with everyone, not just him, but the owner and the other employees, even the other dancers. The women made their money by giving private dances in a small VIP room through a velvet curtain at the back of the bar; Amber was one of the most successful in getting the men to go with her to that room. When she approached the customers, she was friendly, smiling and outgoing – the total opposite of her usual demeanor. Her technique was also the total opposite of the other girls, who were aggressive, rubbing themselves against the men, touching them provocatively, and making overt sexual comments to them. Amber would smile and compliment the men on their looks, and ask them about themselves. She might touch them lightly on the arm, but only after engaging them in conversation. Her come-on line was asking them if they wanted to "go talk somewhere more private." Daryl could see why her approach was effective. She was role-playing, treating the men as if she was a girl who'd just met them in a bar and found them irresistible.

Her sweet-as-molasses, girl-next-door act worked most of the time, but as the word got out that the only strip club for a hundred miles had opened in Alpine, the bar attracted a more diverse clientele. It became a popular locale for bachelor parties, but also a stop-off for a wilder crowd in the summer as bikers passed through on their way to or from the rally in Sturgis. The owner hired professional bouncers for weekends as the small-town bar re-invented itself into a rowdy roadhouse. One evening Daryl watched as Amber approached a heavily-tattooed man who Daryl had already decided to cut-off as he'd been wobbly returning from the washroom. As soon as she started talking to him, the man grabbed at her breast and she reacted as if she'd been stuck with a hot poker. Her knee came up to his groin, and she struck him in the throat with her fist. He doubled over in agony and was quickly grabbed by the bouncers – one gripping each arm – and dragged outside. Impressed by Amber's maneuvers, Daryl realized there was another side to her that he hadn't seen.

Over the next week, Daryl repeatedly tried to engage her, even more intrigued now that she'd shown this street-smart side, but she remained polite and distant. One afternoon when business was slow, Daryl asked her opinion of a new cocktail he'd invented, a "Teton Tequila Sunrise."

"It's good, but a little too strong for me," she said, her voice as soft and sweet as lemon meringue pie.

"Amber, where are you from? You don't sound like you grew up around here."

"No, I grew up in Tennessee. My mama moved out here when I was in high school." She glanced at the brochure for the seminar that Daryl had spread out on the bar. "Are you going to school there?"

Daryl explained the thesis of *Inventing Yourself*, omitting where he'd discovered the book in the first place. He told her about the seminar and took a chance.

"Why don't you come with me? It would be a great opportunity for you to learn more about the system." He smiled and tried to pour on the charm. "I've been saving for a year now to start my own business, and this might be it. I'm out of here when I find the right investment opportunity."

Her demeanor changed when he made his pitch. "I'm sorry, Daryl. I don't date anyone I work with, or my customers. It's just my policy. I'm trying to keep my life simple right now. My mama depended on a man, followed him cross country, and then he dumped her. I'm not going to do that. I'm saving all my tips, and I hope I can buy a small house soon." She could see his face drop, and she added. "I'm sure you're a great guy."

"Amber, I wasn't hitting on you. It's a weekend thing, but we'd get separate rooms. I just thought it might be something you'd be interested in."

She smiled, and it was the first smile he'd seen that wasn't for a customer. "Thanks, Daryl, it's sweet of you to think of me."

Daryl was depressed for the rest of the day. He hadn't tried to date anyone since he'd gotten out of prison. He'd just now had a door slammed in his face.

A week later Daryl was headed home after the closing shift on Saturday night, and as he was opening the door to his camper in the parking lot, he noticed two burly men with Amber, escorting her toward the motel next door. One of the men had Amber by the arm and she kept trying to yank it away, her face contorted with anger. He could see that Amber was favoring her right foot as the men led her on, and he could hear the three of them were arguing, but he couldn't make out a word any of them were shouting. He put his keys in his pocket and jogged quickly over to them, stopping about ten feet away. "Is there a problem? Amber, are these guys bothering you?"

The biggest of the men had to be six-five and over three hundred pounds. He was wearing a Harley tank top, showing off tattooed forearms as hard as anvils. "Mind your own business, buddy. There ain't nothin' to see here."

Daryl persisted. "Amber, are you OK?"

Amber shook her head in fury, but before she could speak, the other man, short and stocky with a bushy beard, took hold of her other arm and shook her into silence. She fell back against the stocky man, clearly unable to support her weight on the injured foot, as the taller man stepped forward. "Get the fuck out of my face. I'm not going to tell you again, asshole."

Daryl stepped around him and punched the stocky one hard in the chest. He was as surprised at Daryl's aggression as Daryl was and stumbled to the ground, releasing his grip on Amber's arm.

"Amber, run!" Daryl shouted. Amber stood still for a split second, weighing her options – "I said *run*, Amber!" – before she took off, limping as fast as she could go toward the motel office.

Daryl turned to face the big man. He never saw the man's face, just his fist coming straight for his head like a concrete block. He was unconscious before the back of his head bounced off the asphalt. The two men took turns kicking his helpless body, their work boots landing blow after blow to his ribs, the pain bringing him back to consciousness. Daryl tried to cover his sides with his arms in a futile attempt at self-defense, so the bigger man turned his attention to Daryl's head and landed two thudding blows to his face.

As Daryl blacked out again, the smaller of the men grabbed the other by the back of his tank top. "Stop. You don't want to kill him. He's out."

When Daryl woke up in the hospital, he was alone and disoriented, but his bladder was ready to burst. When he pulled himself up from the hospital bed, he felt stabbing pain in both sides of his chest, but he crawled over the side and baby-stepped to the bathroom to relieve himself. He didn't recognize the figure in the bathroom mirror. His head looked like a purple balloon sporting two black eyes and a nose swollen into a potato.

The nurse appeared at his door. "Mr. Fay, you're not supposed to be out of bed with those broken ribs." She helped him back into bed and gave him a pill that sent him back into a painless void.

When he awoke, an out-of-focus, blonde-haired angel was rubbing his hand. "My hero is awake."

He blinked several times and the angel's image sharpened. "I've seen myself in the mirror, Amber. I don't look much like a hero." His face hurt with each word he spoke. "Are you OK? Were you able to get away from those guys?"

"Yes, thanks to you. I ran into the hotel office and called the police." She saw a hopeful glance flicker in Daryl's eyes. "No, the police couldn't catch them. They took off right after they were done with you." She touched his face and the pain felt wonderful to him.

"Your foot? They'd already hurt you – "

Amber nodded. "Tripped me on my way out the back door. But it was just a sprain." She shrugged. "I'm fine now, but I couldn't have fought them off on my own. Not with a bum foot. Thank you, Daryl. No one has ever put their life on the line for me before. I owe you big time."

Daryl tried to smile back but could manage only a grimace. "You don't owe me anything. I was really worried when I saw you in the parking lot. Those guys were in the bar earlier… they're real scumbags. I'm glad you were able to get away."

Then he remembered something. "That seminar next Saturday in Salt Lake. I don't want to miss it, and I might need a little help getting around. Would you consider going with me?"

Amber thought for a moment. "OK. We could do that. But it's not a date, right? It's a business opportunity that you want to show me."

He suddenly felt a lot better. "Absolutely. Not a date. We'll get separate rooms and everything."

Daryl's face was still a swollen mess when Amber picked him up for the five-hour drive to Salt Lake City. On the way, Daryl came clean with his life story. He figured he had nothing to lose – and there might never be another occasion when his good deeds might offset the bad things he was going to tell her about himself. And he told her everything – his teenage problems, his mental disorder, his crimes, and his prison time. "I want you to know, I'm not that person now. I've been on the straight and narrow since I got out of prison. And Andrew Adler changed my whole life."

Amber laughed.

Daryl slid his eyes over to her in the driver's seat. "Was my story funny?"

"No," Amber replied quickly, "it's not that it's funny at all. I'm laughing at myself. I said I was done with men. My daddy left my mama before I was born. Her other men walked out on her, too. Men have always only wanted one thing from her – and from me. And I guess I take after my mama – all my boyfriends have been assholes. At least those assholes I dance for now pay me to do it. Now I met you, and I'm thinking maybe you aren't an asshole." Her face suddenly changed, and she stared out the windshield. "Are you going to disappoint me, too?"

"Amber, I think I figured out one thing. The only way I can't disappoint someone else, is to not disappoint myself. I've disappointed myself my whole life, and I'm working on that real hard."

The seminar was held in the grand ballroom at the Regency Hyatt, just off Temple Square in downtown Salt Lake City. Greeters wearing "Eternal Vitality Self-Made" tee shirts and the earnest smiles of the newly converted checked them in at the table outside the ballroom. At the back of the crystal-chandeliered room stood a six-foot bronze statue entitled "Self-made Man." The figure was of a nude man with a hammer and chisel in hand, his bust fully formed, sculpting the lower half of his own body out of a block of granite. Daryl put his arm around Amber. "This is what it's about. Not finding ourselves, but inventing ourselves. We can do this."

They sat through two days of indoctrination into Adler's Self-Creation Methodology, and Daryl and Amber had dinner together each night. She seemed to relax, was cheerful and smiling, and Daryl lost himself in her angelic face and her melodic sweet southern drawl. But he couldn't help wondering: *Was she playing a role with him?* He didn't know, but he wanted her to be sure he wasn't playing one with her. He kept to his word about separate motel rooms, and he refrained from any romantic overtures. It was actually almost enough for him just to be in her presence, to have the opportunity of budding friendship.

On the third morning of the seminar they were presented with Adler's "Investment Opportunity," which involved purchasing a distributorship for a line of nutritional supplements, and health and beauty products called Eternal Vitality or "EV". It was a typical multi-level marketing business model with the real money coming from recruiting a downline of other distributors who would purchase their products from you, and so on. For twenty-five thousand dollars – with a down payment of $10,000 and a five-year installment loan for the balance – a regional distributorship could be yours. For this price you'd receive training, monthly group coaching, and a starter inventory kit.

At lunch, Amber looked at Daryl with a gleam in her eye. "What do you think? Want to become partners?"

Daryl was pleased but surprised. "I'd love to, but I haven't saved enough cash to do this yet."

Amber's eyes twinkled. "I have." She paused as the waiter refilled their water glasses, and then continued. "I'll tell you what. I'll put down the cash, and you work the business."

Daryl laughed. "Aren't you saving for a house?"

Amber shrugged. "Well, maybe we can rent one, and buy a house when the business starts bringing in enough money."

"*We*? I thought you wanted to be partners. *Business* partners. What are you saying? That we should rent a house together?"

"Daryl" – Amber leaned over the table, toward him – "I have a secret. I know you've been watching me since I started dancing at the bar. I was attracted to you... and I wasn't going to let you know – it really is my policy not to date my co-workers. But I've been watching you, too. You treat me different than anyone I've met before. And the way you took on those bikers in the parking lot, no one has ever done anything like that for me. You told me your story on the way here, and I could see we're the same. We're both looking for a better life. And since we've been here, you've been a perfect gentleman. Maybe we could… reinvent ourselves together."

Daryl was speechless – this was not what he was expecting. He struggled with his thoughts and sputtered, "How do we know if we have… you know…chemistry. We haven't even kissed. Shit, we haven't even held hands."

Amber smiled the biggest smile he'd seen since he'd met her. "Right. So we have a lot of ground to make up, don't we?"

She left her side of the booth and joined him on his side. She took his face in her hands. "I know your face is still sore. I promise to be gentle," she said, as she kissed him ever so softly on the lips.

OLD ACE

For Loyd and Rosemary

O ld Ace lay sleeping on a flannel blanket in the corner of the wood-paneled living room, but when Loyd Carson took his field coat and cap from the closet, the dog's ears perked, and he soldiered up to attention. They hadn't been on a hunt this year, but Ace managed to wag his tail, aroused by the fragrance of gunpowder residue on the well-worn jacket, and he didn't notice when Loyd neglected to take his shotgun down from the rack. His eyesight was pretty much gone, and his once dark-brown muzzle, now as white as Loyd's full head of hair, bristled with excitement. At fifteen, he was the longest-lived English Setter Loyd had ever owned. Ace was a house dog now, and the only dog Loyd had ever permitted to sleep indoors. Loyd had a deep fondness for the setters and pointers he bred, but they were working dogs; he disdained the tiny ankle-biters that guarded suburban sofas. He regarded them as an abomination of the wolf genome.

Together they limped down the steps of the back porch past the long-abandoned kennels at the back of the house, and Loyd helped Ace up into the front seat of his truck. Ace hesitated and tried to turn his body away; he knew his spot was in the dog crate in the back. "It's OK, Ace," said Loyd. "Today you're getting special treatment."

They drove five miles down the highway, turning off onto a gravel road for two more miles to reach Loyd's hunting grounds. He'd hunted there for the last fifty years, the first twenty-five with permission of a farmer who let him hunt there in exchange for some of Loyd's game, then after the farmer died, he'd been shocked when his lowball bid at auction had been accepted. The hundred-twenty-acre parcel hadn't attracted much interest, probably because half of it was unfarmable wetlands, swampy groves and steep culverts, with a creek running through it that flooded every spring, a perfect home for quail and pheasant, and even a few wild turkeys. The other half he leased out to a local farmer for a share of his corn crop. Most years the arrangement had ended up giving him a pretty good return on his investment.

Loyd and the dog exited the truck and took their time walking across the stubble on the recently harvested field down the slope toward Cottonwood Creek. Loyd realized how much he'd missed it, the long walks in the woods with just him and his dog. His hunting tastes were limited to upland game birds – the plentiful quail, pheasant and wild turkey; although he liked the more generous meat from duck and goose, he was too restless to sit in a boat for hours, and there was something about killing large game, mainly white-tailed deer in southern Illinois, that struck him as vulgar. Loyd ate what he killed, and he considered trophy hunting akin to blood lust.

Ace suddenly came alive, his nose in the air, and he tried to run, but hobbled more than trotted down the steep grade, stopping periodically to sniff for scents in the wet, black soil. Loyd lost sight of him down a culvert a hundred yards away. As he hurried after him, he cursed his hip, which he was scheduled to have replaced after the first of the year, and followed Ace's trail. He found him on the other side of a thicket of cottonwoods, Ace standing on point, still as a marble statue in a bird-scented trance. He knew Ace would hold point until he released him, for hours if necessary. Once a sixteen-point buck had loped between Ace and a hidden covey when he was on point and it didn't faze him. Stopping about ten yards from Ace, he could see he was struggling, his left hind leg trembling badly. Loyd whistled, relieving Ace from his pose, and they continued on, skirting the clump of brush so as not to flush the game Ace had so artfully located.

It was a beautiful November morning, bright and crisp as a starched dress shirt, and Loyd could see the creek was running high, nearly up to the bench on the bank that he'd crafted from downed trees years ago. They sat together, and as he pulled a rawhide bone from his pocket and placed it near Ace's mouth, Loyd thought about the year that Ace was born.

It was during Loyd's last year as principal of Godfrey High School, a position he'd held for over twenty years. He was at the farm, having taken the morning off for some dental work, and was stopping to pick up his share of the crop check on his way back to school, when he heard a gunshot out the open window of his truck. He drove a piece down the country road looking into the wooded section of his land when he spotted Glen McDonald, carrying a rifle in his elbow, and holding a dead squirrel by the tail in his other hand. Loyd knew Glen well, as he did most of the three hundred students in the small rural high school. Glen had one of the highest IQ scores in the school but was a chronic truant, and Loyd knew there was a chance he wouldn't graduate. He lived with his single mother who worked nights at a local bar and slept all day.

The next morning, Loyd had called Glen into his office during his study hall period. Glen was a tall, skinny boy, with a mop of coal black hair and deep-set black eyes that gave him a bit of a haunted look. He was dressed in dirty blue jeans and a ripped Garth Brooks tee shirt. Loyd studied him for a moment. His long face was beet red from an acne outbreak, and he made a mental note to have the school nurse see if she could do something about it.

"Glen, have a seat."

Glen looked down as he shuffled his feet. "Am I in trouble, Mr. Carson?"

"Just have a seat, Glen. Let's talk," said Loyd.

Glen reluctantly sat in the chair in front of the principal's desk but continued to look down. Loyd stood up and took the chair next to Glen. "Glen look at me."

Glen looked up and Loyd held his gaze. "We have a problem. Actually, we have a couple of problems. I know you skipped school yesterday."

"I was sick, I brought a note in from my mom."

"Stop. Let's make a deal with each other right now. You stop lying to me, and I'm going to try to help you. I want you to graduate and right now there's a very good chance you won't. But you have to promise not to lie. Let's be straight with each other. Understand?"

"Yes. I understand."

"OK. So, you were skipping school yesterday, right?"

"Yes, sir."

"Why have you been skipping school so much, Glen?"

"Well, there's a lot of reasons. I have to help my mom… And – "

Loyd interrupted. "Remember our promise. Be straight with me."

"I guess I just don't like school," the boy spat.

Loyd nodded. "Well, you must like math and science. You're getting As in trig and physics."

"Yes, I like those subjects."

"And you don't like English and Spanish – right now you're failing those. You know you need to pass those to graduate. Do you want to graduate, Glen?"

"Yes, sir. I want to graduate."

"How's your mother going to feel if you don't graduate? Do you know how hard she works so you can go to school? You need to think about that."

"I know. It would kill her. I'm just not very good at English or Spanish, though."

"Well, you're wrong about that, Glen. I don't think it's because you're not good at those subjects. It's that you've missed a lot of school. The only reason you're getting As in math and science is that those are easy for you. The other subjects you have to work at and you're not willing to do that, are you?"

"I'm not lazy, Mr. Carson. I work after school five days a week at Albertson's grocery store. I just don't have the time."

"You had time yesterday to take the day off to hunt squirrels though, didn't you?"

Glen didn't respond.

"Did you have permission from the owner of that land to hunt there? Now tell the truth."

"No, I didn't. But those two squirrels I got yesterday, we had one for dinner, and froze the other one. My mom and I eat the rabbits and squirrels I get."

Loyd sighed. "I have to decide what to do with you, Glen." He paused and gave Glen his sternest look before continuing. "Tomorrow you're going to come to my office before school, and you're going to give me the answers to three questions. Do you want to graduate? Are you willing to do the work to make that happen? And can you take a solemn oath to not ditch school the rest of the year? The answers to those three questions are going to determine how I handle this. Do you understand?"

"Yes, sir." As Glen left the office, he glanced at the large wooden paddle with holes drilled on the face hanging on the wall of the principal's office. It was there for intimidation, but Loyd had never actually used it on any student, and he'd never consider using it on Glen. That would be letting him off easy.

That afternoon Loyd talked to Glen's Spanish and English teachers. The Spanish teacher was cooperative and arranged for a tutor for Glen during his study hall to catch up. The English teacher, who was also the wrestling coach, was problematic.

"Loyd, Glen has already failed the class. He's missed three exams and hasn't turned in most of the assignments. I'm sure you know that most of these absences are unexcused. I've lost two of my best wrestlers this year for academic reasons, and I'm not about to cut this kid a break. He isn't even trying."

Loyd went back to his office and thought about the problem. He wasn't willing to give up on Glen yet. If the English instructor wouldn't cooperate, his only option would be to withdraw him from the class and enroll him in an independent study but, he wondered, would that be enough? Glen was obviously very smart, but his home life had been chaotic, and he'd been turned off by school early on. His record throughout grade school and middle school had been the same: academic success when he applied himself, but self-sabotage through constant truancy. What would make a difference this time?

The next morning Loyd looked up when Glen walked into his office, right on time. "Have you thought about our conversation?" Loyd asked him.

"I have, Mr. Carson. I know it will be terrible for my mom if I don't graduate. So, yes, I want to graduate. I will do whatever I need to do to pass English and Spanish. And I won't skip school for the test of the year. I promise."

Loyd looked at Glen and knew it was impossible to tell if he was sincere, but he felt he had to give him every opportunity to prove he was. "Good. Now sit down. I have a proposal for you. I understand you like to hunt rabbits and squirrels. Have you ever hunted birds?"

"I'd love to hunt birds, Mr. Carson, but I don't have a shotgun, just a twenty-two rifle."

"Well, Glen, I like to hunt pheasant and quail with my hunting dogs. And I can loan you a shotgun. Would you like to come with me some time?"

"I'd love that."

"I'm going to make you a deal. I've arranged for a Spanish tutor for you instead of study hall for the rest of the year. As far as your English class is concerned, I'm withdrawing you from Mr. Webster's class. Instead, you will come to my office every day, and you will have your English class with me as independent study. I'll be able to see firsthand how serious you are about keeping your promise. If you do, I'll take you hunting with me. How does that sound?"

"That sounds amazing, Mr. Carson. Thank you."

They met every morning for the rest of the school year, with Loyd continually holding out the carrot of hunting expeditions. Taking into account Glen's interest in nature, Loyd started his class with *A River Runs Through It*, and then they moved on to *Call of the Wild*, and Glen seemed to enjoy the books and their discussions about them. Loyd was surprised that Glen actually was a competent writer, and his grammar and spelling were surprisingly proficient. At that point, Loyd took Glen hunting for the first time.

Glen was a natural hunter. He was adept with his twenty-two but had to transition to using Loyd's twenty-gauge shotgun which had a much stronger recoil. He worked with Glen on gun safety, demonstrating that the boy's customary elbow carry with his twenty-two was not safe when hunting with others or in brush where the muzzle could be caught and misdirected. He showed

Glen how to read the land for nesting areas for quail and pheasant, and how to handle his hunting dog, Queenie.

On a particularly fruitful day – they had brought back two pheasant and several quail – Loyd invited Glen to dinner at his house. Loyd supervised Glen as he dressed the birds on the butchering table that Loyd had set up in the garage, showing him how to double-check the carcasses for any buckshot. Loyd's wife and daughters would get very annoyed when they came across a random piece of lead in their bird. They gave the birds to Loyd's wife, Rosemary, to roast. At the dining table, Loyd and Rosemary sat at each end, and Glen was flanked by the Loyd's two oldest daughters on one side of the table while the two youngest sat on the other side eyeing the strange young man.

Loyd had to remind Glen to wash up for dinner, and Glen didn't seem to have the least idea of table manners. When he started to eat before Loyd offered grace, Loyd's daughter Marcia put her hand on Glen's arm to stop him.

That evening, after Glen had gone home, Loyd's youngest daughter, Paula, interrogated him. "Why did you need to bring him to dinner? He's really strange."

"Well, Paula, I'm trying to help him out. He comes from a bro…" Loyd almost said "broken home," and caught himself. "Glen is being raised by a single mom. He doesn't have a father in his home, and they don't have much money. I'm helping him in his studies. He was in danger of not graduating, and now he's doing much better."

"Well, he talks with his mouth full. It's disgusting."

"His mom works all the time. He doesn't have someone like your mother to teach him table manners. You have to be understanding of his situation."

"But you don't do this for all of your students. You've never brought any of the others to dinner."

Loyd thought about this. Why *had* he brought him to dinner?

After he saw how much Glen enjoyed hunting, Loyd decided to accelerate the difficulty of his class. When he found out that Glen also had an interest in history, they moved on to *All Quiet on the Western Front*," and *The Winds of War*. Loyd felt a sense of pride when Glen decided to read the sequel, *War and Remembrance*, on his own. They finished the school year with *A Tale of Two Cities*, and then *Hamlet*, because Loyd could not allow him to graduate without exposure to Shakespeare.

One day when they were sitting in Loyd's truck after the hunt, Loyd asked Glen what he planned on doing after graduation. Glen thought for a moment. "I think I'll try to get on at the food-processing plant down by the river."

"Have you thought of college?"

"I can't really afford that."

"I couldn't afford college either, Glen. I worked my way through. It took me a few years longer, but I'm glad I did. I come from a family of farmers, and I'm the first person in my family to go to college. You have the brains to do something more with your life. Maybe you could go to community college for the first two years then transfer. You could do work-study, and you'd end up with a much better life for you and your family."

"I hadn't thought it was a possibility, really."

"Well, think about it. I can get together with your counselor and I'm sure we can figure out a plan for you."

Glen's counselor was Mary Lou Austin and she came into Loyd's office a few days later. "I hear you've been putting ideas in Glen McDonald's head about college."

"I talked to him about it and told him you could help him with applications."

"Do you really think that's a good idea. He's barely making it through high school."

"I think you should check his grades and attendance again. He hasn't missed a day in months, and he's now getting a B+ in English and a C in Spanish. He's a smart kid. I think we should help him if that's what he wants to do."

"Why are you so interested in him? I've met with him many times, and he hates school. I don't know why you think he could be successful in college. We have some plumbing apprenticeships available in Alton. Wouldn't he be better suited for that?"

"His attitude has changed, Mary Lou. I've seen his potential. I think he can do more than clean out sewers for a living. Do me a favor and help him, OK?"

Queenie had a litter of six puppies that spring, and Loyd had sold all but the runt of the litter. When Loyd and Glen got back to Loyd's house after fishing at Cottonwood Creek, Paula and the puppy were in the backyard, playing tug of war, and Glen asked if he was the only one left.

"Yes, he is," said Loyd."

"Have you told him, yet?" asked Paula.

"No, honey. Why don't you tell him?"

Paula held the puppy out to Glen, who laughed as the dog licked his face.

"Glen, this is Ace. He's your graduation present," Paula said.

It took Glen a moment to process. "What did you say?"

"He's your graduation present. If you want him," said Loyd.

"Of course I do! Thank you so much," said Glen as Ace squirmed in his arms.

Loyd retired at the end of the school year, and Glen was busy the next year working full-time while taking a full load at the community college, and he crossed paths with Loyd only on occasion. On a fall day the year after that, Glen called and asked Loyd if he was available to hunt. As Loyd pulled his truck into his parking place at the farm, he saw Glen's beat-up Ford already parked there. Glen got out of his truck and opened the door, and a beautiful liver-and-white English setter bounded out.

"Hi, Mr. Carson. Easy now, Ace," said Glen.

"Glen, it's good to see you. How has Ace turned out for you?"

"He's been a great companion, Mr. Carson. I've been training him when I have time, and I think he's coming along well." Glen fumbled in his pocket and pulled out an envelope. "I have something to show you."

Loyd took the envelope and pulled out the letter. When he saw the shield logo at the top of the page, his heart skipped a beat. "You've been accepted at Eastern Illinois University?" He asked it as a question, even though he'd just read the words.

"I sure have. I got it yesterday, but I wanted to tell you in person."

"You know that's my alma mater."

"Of course I do." Glen laughed. "Why do you think I applied there?"

Loyd looked down at Ace, afraid looking at Glen's face would overwhelm him. He managed to say, "That's really great news. Have you decided on a major?"

"Math education. I'm going to be a high-school math teacher."

"That's wonderful, Glen. I'm so happy for you." He gave Glen a quick embrace. "Now let's celebrate with a pheasant and a quail or two."

"They hunted together that day, but it was different. Glen was no longer the skinny, disheveled kid from high school. He'd become a well-spoken confident young man in just a little more than a year. Loyd had been an educator his whole life, and it had been a frustrating task at times, with the pay hardly enough to raise a family, and he'd rarely seen tangible fruit from his work. But here it was. Glen was his legacy.

Loyd didn't see or hear from Glen again for more than two years, and when he hunted alone now, he thought about his daughters. He was now seeing more and more female hunters in the woods, and he wondered why he'd never invited his daughters into this world. They'd never really liked eating game. Was that the reason? But they did enjoy loading his shotgun shells at the dining room table. He felt a pang of regret. The world had changed around him, and he was more able to accept women in traditionally male roles now than he'd been years ago. He loved his daughters and realized he'd missed out on knowing them in a different way. He also thought of Glen, and he wondered how he was doing.

Then one November, early in the new century, he was sitting on his front porch cleaning his gun when Glen pulled up in the same old truck he'd been driving for years. He got out and walked over to the porch holding Ace by his leash.

"Glen, how are you? I haven't seen you for so long. Sit down, let's catch up."

Glen sat down on the chair next to him. "How's school?" Loyd asked.

"School is going really well, Mr. Carson. I made the Dean's list last semester." Then he paused and a shadow crossed his face. "But I've decided to enlist. It's just something I need to do. After what's happened, I can't stay here and go to school."

Loyd felt his heart pound in his chest. "I know how you feel, son. But I wish you'd give this some more thought."

"I've thought of nothing else since September eleventh. You should know how I feel. You enlisted and went to Viet Nam."

"Yes, but that was different. We know now that was a mistake. All those thousands of lives lost for nothing."

"That's not like this, Mr. Carson. Our country was attacked. On our own soil this time. And we need to go get those responsible."

Loyd didn't have an answer for that, and sat silent, searching for the words that would convince the younger man that this was a terrible idea. But the words wouldn't come.

"Mr. Carson, I need to ask you a big favor. Would you take care of Ace for me until I get back? Mom isn't doing well, and I know she can't handle him while I'm gone."

"Of course, I will," Loyd promised, "but think about it some more, will you?"

"I'm afraid it's already done, Mr. Carson. I report next week."

Glen stood and patted Ace, "You be a good boy for Mr. Carson, Ace. Mr. Carson, I don't know how to thank you for everything you've done for me." Glen held out his hand.

Loyd stood, and instead of taking his hand, he wrapped Glen in a bear hug. "Be careful over there."

Loyd held onto Ace's leash as Glen walked to his truck, and Ace whimpered quietly.

Thirteen months later, Loyd answered a knock on his front door. As soon as he saw her face he knew. He stood on his front porch, his arms wrapped around Sally McDonald as they both sobbed. Sally had no family, so he and Ace sat next to her at Godfrey Veterans' Cemetery as the Methodist minister prayed over Glen's flag-draped casket. Loyd's wife and daughters sat dabbing their eyes in the row behind them. Loyd liked to say he had four beautiful daughters but had never been blessed with the burden of a son. Now he knew he couldn't say that anymore.

Ace gnawed in contented bliss as Loyd reached down and stroked the soft fur on his head, running his hand all the way from the tip of his head to his tail, carefully avoiding the large tumor at the edge of his spine on his hind quarters. Loyd imagined that if things had turned out differently, Glen might be the principal at Godfrey High now, and Ace would be sitting here on the banks of the creek with a different master. Loyd looked at the sky. Dark clouds were rolling in and the wind had picked up, sending a cold chill all the way through him. He shivered and turned his collar up, and pulled his hat down over his ears. Old Ace felt the change too, and dropped his bone and sat up, moving close to Loyd and leaning his body against him. It wouldn't be long now, but at least they'd had a very good day.

TIME TRAVELERS

’m not a sentimental man. If my life were a painting, it wouldn’t be a Norman Rockwell-esque collage of heart-warming experiences painted in bright red, white and blue tones. I grew up in a household of chaos, and I’m a product of that chaos. I’ve never found the need to look back and redefine those years to fit a Hollywood happy ending. I’m a realist. Things are what they are, and you move on. After all, America didn’t advance from sea to shining sea by lamenting its mistakes. So it was to my surprise that I found my thinking redirected to the past as I drove through Canton, Ohio on a rare trip back to my hometown. It was hard not to compare what I was seeing *now* to the town that existed when I graduated from high school thirty years before.

In grammar school, I’d learned that at the turn of the twentieth century Canton had been the proud hometown of President William McKinley, whose martyred bones are still housed there atop a hill in a huge granite mausoleum worthy of an Egyptian Pharaoh, and that during the industrial revolution Canton was the home to several captains of industry, and that the city went on to become one of the meccas of steel manufacturing in northeastern Ohio. The downtown of my childhood was bustling with several movie theaters, high-end department stores, and a vibrant night life. I remembered milkshakes at McCrory's lunch counter on shopping sprees with my mother, and the wonderfully greasy smell of fried burgers on toasted buns served by the uniformed waitresses. I'd seen Hulk Hogan take on all comers at the Canton Auditorium in middle school, and, when I was a teenager, Madonna had been *Crazy For Me* and my friends in the mosh pit there on a hot summer night.

The city was already well into its decline when I graduated from high school, but I'd been too self-involved to notice. Now as I drove into the city center on the way to the Grand McKinley Hotel, I felt I was entering the ruins of Industrial America. The downtown had been made over a couple of times since then; most of the nineteen-thirties architectural gems had been torn down and a few replaced by cheap steel and glass structures, but mostly the downtown was now empty lots, boarded up storefronts, or a hodgepodge of small retail businesses. An empty lot full of homeless men warming themselves from oil drums was only a block from the hotel where I was staying.

When I'd received the invitation for my thirtieth high-school reunion, I'd put it on my desk and ignored it for several weeks, and then one day I started to think back on that time, and made the decision to attend. My friend Gary and I had decided to pre-game before the main event, so I was waiting for him at a high top in the corner of the crowded sports bar next to the ballroom of the Grand McKinley. An insurance convention occupied the hotel that weekend, and the lounge was full of men about our age. I surveyed the crowd of middle-aged middle managers, looking for a familiar face. Not that I knew for sure I'd recognize Gary; it'd been over twenty years since I'd seen my old high-school debate partner, at his second wedding. I had been between marriages then, and he and his bride had a full schedule, so we hadn't spent any one-on-one time together. Since then our contacts had been limited to a call each year on our birthdays to catch up. A tall man, with a scholarly salt-and-pepper beard came through the door, and I tentatively waved him over. When he was a few feet away, I recognized Gary's same lopsided smile from all those years ago. Neither of us had ever been particularly in touch with our feelings back in the day, but I greeted him this evening with a warm embrace.

"Dave, I was afraid you'd never recognize me with all these people," he said.

"Oh, it wasn't hard. I just looked for the guy who looked least like an insurance salesman." Actually, I'd been looking for a middle-aged man who looked most like an academic, and in his corduroy sport coat and thick glasses, Gary looked a stereotype of what he was, a professor of Political Science at William and Mary.

Gary chuckled and volunteered, "I recognized you by your smirk." I knew exactly what he meant. My first wife had threatened more than once to 'knock that shit-eating smirk' off my face." The truth is, I wasn't *always* smirking. I was cursed with a resting smirk face, which had gotten me into many jams with the women in my life and resulted in more than a few late-night altercations in barrooms.

Gary gestured at the shot glasses on the table, neatly arranged in parallel brushed nickel racks. "What's this?"

"They're running a special tonight on bourbon flights. I remembered that's your drink."

He put his palm out in faux trepidation. "Ooh, are you sure about this? Don't you remember what happened last time? Your wife was really annoyed when she had to bail us out that night." He seemed for a moment to match my smirk. "I guess I should say your ex-wife."

"That seems like a lifetime ago, but we're a bit more mature now, don't you think? Besides this is a special evening." When I'd gotten the invitation to our thirtieth high school reunion, I'd given him a call, but he was reluctant.

"Look," he'd said. "High school had more low points that high points for both of us, and to be honest,

I really have nothing to say to any of those people. I wouldn't mind seeing you, though."

I lived in Chicago now, and Gary lived in Virginia, but he still had family in Canton, Ohio. I got the impression that he wanted me to talk him into it.

"I hear you," I'd told him. "Our high-school experiences were … mixed. Let's get together and hang out. We can cruise the reunion and check out early and go to a bar if it's too bad."

Sitting now at the bar, I eyed his professorial uniform. "What's with the duds? I thought we had an agreement. You're looking very formal tonight."

"Oh, right," he laughed. The invitation had specified dress as "Comfortably Casual" and we'd discussed during our telephone call what that term would mean to the folks in Canton. We decided: white wife-beaters, pajama bottoms, flip flops with bathrobes, and it might be fun to arrive fashionably late for a Big Lebowski-style entrance.

I'd always been able to make him laugh. Gary was more serious than me in just about every area of his life, but we'd made a great debate team. Gary would give the well thought-out and researched academic argument, and I'd be the attack dog, poking holes in our opponents' arguments with an entertaining combination of sardonic wit and biting ridicule. Once I'd reduced a member of the other team to tears when I'd gotten an admission during cross-examination that part of their speech had been plagiarized from an episode of "Matlock." I'd made the point that it wasn't so much the plagiarism that was appalling, but the quality of the source. We lost that debate because the judge had said I had been "unnecessarily cruel."

"How's the real estate market looking?" asked Gary.

I'd jumped from one job to another and one relationship to another for the last thirty years. I'd always known that I would have been a great trial attorney, juries would have appreciated my killer instinct more than high-school debate judges, but the truth is that I was too undisciplined for law school. I'd taught high-school English after college, then with a couple of little ones, decided I needed to make more money and became a stockbroker. When the internet tech boom busted at the turn of the century, I became a real estate broker, and for the last decade I'd been doing fairly well flipping houses.

"Flipping works well in up markets and in down markets. It's not like the TV shows, though. I'm doing all right." I quickly changed the subject; the last thing I wanted to do was compare my sketchy job history with Gary's academic credentials. "Let's make a dent in this bourbon and get loosened up for the evening."

Each of our flights consisted of five half-shot glasses of premium bourbons, and we used them to toast our deceased classmates. Our high school was both racially and economically diverse, about a third of our class was African American, and about eighty percent of our class was blue collar, and, thirty years later, nearly twenty percent of our class hadn't made it to middle age. The diseases of the working class: cancer, diabetes, heart disease, opioid addiction, were the primary culprits. Gary toasted our most famous graduate, Nate Watson, who'd been an NBA star but had succumbed to a rare disease just a few years after retiring. We both toasted a mutual friend who'd fallen off a mountain in Colorado, and then Gary toasted Carolyn Manning.

My heart skipped. "Carolyn is dead?"

"She died of breast cancer last month," Gary said. "My sister sent me her obituary. I meant to call you."

My mood suddenly changed. "You know how I felt about her. I was looking forward to seeing her again." I took a sip of my drink, and the finality of it washed over me. "I never got to say goodbye."

Carolyn was the love my life. I fell in love in second grade when she taught me how to write my name in cursive. I'd thought we were a couple because we were the only two members of the class that could write that way.

I sighed. "You know I never really gave up on her. I asked her to be my girlfriend more than once, and she declined every time. But she did it so sweetly that it always made me think the timing just wasn't right – that I still had a chance. I didn't realize how thoughtful she was until many years later."

"But wasn't she giving you false hope? Wouldn't it have been better just to tell you that you had no chance?"

"Oh, my friend, you haven't figured out yet that false hope is better than no hope at all." I finished my last demi-shot with a heavy heart. "How are you feeling?"

"Mellow, very mellow," Gary said.

I'd started to feel the effects of the bourbon, but with the news of Carolyn suddenly weighing on me, I knew I needed something more. "Me too, but mellow isn't the feeling I really need this evening. Hold out your hand."

I reached in my pocket and dropped two gummy bears into Gary's palm.

"What's this?' said Gary.

"Edibles. Straight from Colorado. Take one now and one in about an hour to keep the buzz going the whole evening." Since college, booze had been my choice for self-medication, but recently I'd found that edibles were easier on my newly sensitive stomach than alcohol.

Gary eyed the tiny purple troll-shaped edibles skeptically. "I'm not sure about this."

"Hey, we're not driving. Trust me, this strain is amazing. And I don't know about you, but I'm not going in there unless I'm high."

The ballroom had seen better days, as had almost everything in Canton. Built in the nineteen-sixties, when northeastern Ohio was the mecca of steel manufacturing, the ballroom's worn carpeting and chandelier that was missing a few crystals were symbols of what had happened to the area since then. The room was enlivened only slightly by Huey Lewis echoing from the disc jockey's giant speakers, and the huge red-and-black banner welcoming the "Canton McKinley Class of 1986".

"Oh, shit." said Gary. "There's John Whitman."

A gaunt, spider-armed man dressed in a black suit and sporting a scraggly black beard was meandering in our direction. "Damn, he looked like a skinny nerd in high school, but now he looks a lot like Abe Lincoln," I said.

"John does one-man Lincoln shows at Civil War festivals and county fairs on weekends," said Gary. "It's quite popular in Virginia." If I hadn't known that Gary rarely cracked wise about anything, I would have thought he was joking.

Gary and John had been rivals throughout high school, and Gary had barely beaten John out for vale-dictorian of our class. John was a professor of American History at University of Virginia, and their academic rivalry had continued throughout their careers.

Abe spied us and walked over. "Do you know what Lincoln's middle name was?"

Gary put out his hand and John shook it. The gummy bear was starting to kick in, and the scene reminded me of a painting of Lincoln shaking hands with Stephen Douglas.

When Gary didn't answer his question, Abe looked Gary dead in the eye. "He didn't have a middle name."

"Good to see you, John. I think I might have come up with that if you'd given me a moment," said Gary.

John nodded somewhat formally. "Professor Elliot, I really enjoyed your paper on *Polk, U.S. Colonialism and the Mexican American War*. It was good enough to be published in one of *our* journals."

I could see Gary's face change, wounded by the insult. John considered political science to be a less rigorous academic discipline than American history.

Gary didn't mince words and went right in for the kill. "How's the shoulder, John?"

Gary had tackled John in a sandlot football game our senior year and severely injured John's shoulder. He'd needed surgery and had missed a substantial amount of school. It was likely the reason that Gary beat him out for valedictorian.

"Shoulder's fine. Can't believe you still remember that."

"He brags about it all the time," I piled on.

"I see you brought your court jester with you," said John, still looking at Gary and not acknowledging me. "You were king of the nerds back in the day, and you never went anywhere without your friend."

"John, what's with the suit?" I said. "This was supposed to be comfortably casual."

"When Lincoln removes the stove pipe hat, he's comfortably casual," said Gary. I knew he was pissed.

John moved along. I looked at Gary. "Nice quip, but I think we should mingle. "Together, it could get dangerous for our classmates."

We separated, and to the left of the room I noticed five members of the state championship swim team. They'd been inseparable in high school and always traveled in a group, perhaps because the lean, smooth-shaven swimmers were targets of the hairy macho football players. They had been speaking to a couple at a table, and I watched as all five moved as one – like a school of middle-aged flounder – to another table and started talking to the people seated there.

I went to the bar and got a bourbon and soda, and encountered Ken Horton, former President of Young Republicans. He was wearing a red and black tie and sporting a Trump 2016 badge on his lapel. "Dave, I'm glad you're here. This your first reunion?' "It is," I said. "I thought I should come to one before we start dropping like flies."

"I've been to every one of them." Then with a gleam in his eye he said, "You're for Hillary, I assume."

We were three weeks from the election, and driving in from Chicago I'd seen nothing but Trump signs from Valparaiso, Indiana all the way to Canton. I no longer believed the national polls. My polling data was signs staked in the ground for mile after mile on the thoroughfares of the Midwest. They were the signs of desperation and false hope, and there was no more desperate place than northeastern Ohio. My father and the fathers of most of my classmates had raised families on middle-class wages while working in the now-shuttered steel factories. Now their children and grandchildren worked minimum wage jobs in a booming economy. I'd researched Ken and a few of my other classmates on social media, and knew he was an executive of one of the companies that had moved manufacturing offshore. I decided to play with him a bit.

"I despise the Clintons. You're probably not going to believe this, but I'm a Trump social media content researcher in the Midwest." I lowered my voice. "You know those rumors about collaborating with the Russians? I'm in charge of finding alt-right news stories to send to them so they can post to millions of fake accounts all over the internet. That wild Pizzagate story about the Clintons and sex trafficking? That was me."

I could see he was intrigued. "Wow, you sure have changed. I always knew you were a smart guy. I'm glad to see that you saw the light. I'm impressed. We're going to show those libtards how it's done. Obama thought he knew something about using the internet in elections. We're going to make what he did look like child's play."

He wasn't the least disturbed that I'd just confessed to colluding with the Russians, so I decided to crank it up a notch. I leaned in closer and talked even softer. "And I'll tell you something else. That supposed video of Trump with the Russian prostitutes in Moscow? It's real. Putin is blackmailing Trump with it. I heard this from someone at the top of the Trump campaign. He spilled it when I took him out one night in Chicago and he got really drunk. I don't know about you, but that doesn't bother me one bit. We're going to get lower taxes and stop subsidizing people that don't want to work for a living. We're going to take our country back."

For a moment I thought I'd gone too far, but he put his arm around me and grinned. "You know what? I thought you were a prick in high school, but you turned out all right. And please post some stories about how the left is trying to turn us all gay. Straight white males are becoming an endangered species. We're going to take our country back from the fags and the lesbos. Keep up the good work." He handed me his card. "Let's keep in touch. If you ever need any help, I would do literally anything to see Trump elected."

"Oh, I believe you would." I reached into my pocket looking for a business card, and suddenly remembered I wasn't actually a Trump foreign operative. I found my second gummy bear and popped it into my mouth.

Feeling a bit dizzy, and although I had no appetite, I knew I needed food. I hadn't eaten all day and the bourbon and the cannabis were starting to work on me. I wandered to the hors d'oeuvres table and filled my plate, all the while looking for a face that I might recognize. I nearly spilled ranch dip all over myself when someone punched me hard in the arm. It was Rachel Greenburg, and her face was as red as her beautiful head of hair.

She pointed her finger at me. "Dave Wolsky, what's this I hear about you working for Trump? You were a socialist the last time we talked."

Rachel was the top extemporaneous speaker on our speech and debate team, and the most politically aware of all of us. "I see you talked to Ken. I was putting him on. I thought I'd see if I could say anything that would be a bridge too far. Apparently, that's not possible. It's clear there are no boundaries. They'll even commit treason to win this election. You don't really believe that I could support Trump, do you?"

"I wouldn't think so, but I haven't talked to you for a long time. And after how you left Denise and that whole thing, who knows?"

Rachel had been my classmate, but my first wife had met her when we were in college, and we had visited with her a few times in the first years after we were married. "So how do you know about that?"

"Well, she wrote me this long letter, sort of a treatise really, giving me her side of the whole sordid story."

It had been a difficult divorce, and a tumultuous time in my life. Still, it was strange that she would write a letter to Rachel. They hadn't been friends really. I wondered how many other letters were out there. This might explain why none of our mutual friends would talk to me after I left. "You know I got married when I was twenty-one. I wasn't ready to be married. Hell, I wasn't ready to be an adult. It doesn't surprise me that Denise kept a dossier on me. I was a terrible husband, and I'm sure whatever she wrote to you is true. She's happy now and much better off without me." Time to change the subject. "And what are you doing these days?"

"This Trump campaign is driving me crazy. I've already seen a half-dozen classmates with MAGA gear on. What really gets to me is that the evangelicals are supporting him. He's the most non-religious candidate ever."

"So, what does a do-gooder Jewish atheist care anyway about the evangelicals?" I asked.

"They believe that anyone who doesn't believe in Jesus is going to hell. As long as you believe in Jesus, nothing else matters. The neo-Nazis say that Hitler is in heaven because he prayed to Jesus before he killed himself. So Hitler may be in heaven, but Jews are in hell?" She was quite worked up over the whole matter.

"I think the evangelicals provide for a Jewish exemption. They believe that Jews can go to heaven without believing in Jesus, but I'm guessing you already know this," I said.

"I don't want a fucking Jewish exemption."

"It seems to me you can have your cake and eat it too here. You're an atheist, but since you're Jewish, you have the exemption. If you're wrong about God and Jesus, you can still get into heaven. Sounds like a pretty good deal to me. And besides," I added, "do you really want to share heaven with Hitler anyway?"

She gave me the look of exasperation that I'd experienced with women my whole life. "Has anyone ever told you that you're an idiot?"

With that I started laughing.

"Why is that so funny?" she said.

"You haven't changed one bit in thirty years. I love that so much. I just want you to know that… I really appreciate you." I started giggling.

"Are you high?"

"A little," I said.

"You should probably get something more to eat than crackers. The speech team has a table if you want to join us for the meal."

I sat with them, but realized I still had no appetite whatsoever, and picked at my rubbery chicken and overcooked broccoli. I no longer had the stomach for small talk or witticisms, and I was starting to feel the anxiety of coming down from the drugs and the booze. I searched my pockets and realized I had no more gummy bears with me.

Gary noticed and whispered, "Are you OK?"

"Isn't it hot in here? I'm going to get some air." I excused myself and went to the cash bar, but it was closed until after the meal, so I went outside. The cool October air felt welcome, but I was still feeling woozy.

And there on a bench, smoking a cigarette, was Lisa Dahl. Lisa was one of the primary reasons I'd felt it necessary to be high for this reunion. Although I'd done many regrettable things in my life, and my transgression with her was not even in the top fifty or so of my sins, for some reason it was the one that bothered me the most. I'd rehearsed what I wanted to say to her for more than thirty years now and had chickened out many times before. After high school, I'd made the excuse to myself that I didn't know how to contact her, but she'd lived in Canton her whole life and it wouldn't have been hard to track her down.

"Hi, Lisa."

She looked up without any sign of recognition and glanced at my name tag. "Hi, Dave."

I took a breath and started right in. I knew if I started with small talk, I'd probably chicken out again. "I want to apologize."

"For what?"

"I should have done this over thirty years ago. There's no excuse, really. I guess I was just ashamed, embarrassed …I just couldn't bring myself to face you."

She looked puzzled. "What is it you're talking about?"

"Ninth grade. Fall dance. I stood you up. It was a terrible thing for me to do. It must have been awful for you. I wish I'd had somebody in my life to tell me not to do it. To tell me it was wrong, to not be a jerk. Unfortunately, I didn't. And even worse, I never owned up to it. So, I'm sorry. There is nothing else I can say. I'm so so sorry."

Her expression was a blank. "It's– It's OK… But, Dave, I have no recollection of this."

I looked at her face, and to me she looked just like the fifteen-year-old girl who I had humiliated, and I felt like crying. How is it possible that she doesn't remember? I know for a fact that she missed the next week of school after the dance, and I'd been shunned the rest of the year by my female classmates. Is it really conceivable that she didn't remember?

"I'm glad. I'm glad you don't remember. But, anyway, I'm sorry. I just wanted to let you know."

"Why, thank you. But really, it was a long time ago."

I walked away and stood inside the door looking at her. She put out her cigarette and opened her purse, took out a tissue and dabbed at her eyes. Did she remember or didn't she? What a narcissistic fool I'd been. I'd had this obsessive self-centered need for confession, for some kind of absolution. What was the real purpose of my self-flagellation? Was carrying around my thirty-year-old guilt providing me with some perverse nobility for acknowledging my villainy? I'd probably just opened up a decades-old wound that had healed over, forcing Lisa to relive the hurt.

Back in the ballroom, I saw Joey Simon sitting by himself in the corner. His head was turning back and forth as if he was scanning the room, and he was muttering to himself. I walked over and sat next to him.

"Hi, Joey, is everything OK?

"Hi Dave," he said. "Kind of crazy, isn't it?"

"It sure is. I'm struggling to process everything myself." Joey hadn't been much of a student. He was a musician, the lead guitar player in a band in high school, but I'd thought of him as the coolest kid in school – he'd been the primary supplier of drugs to our class. I could see that he was still moving his head back and forth, and I asked, "What do you see?"

"I'm trippin'. I dropped some acid before I came tonight. You won't believe what I'm seeing. You want a hit?"

"I'll pass. I'm still a little high on some edibles. I'm too old for anything stronger these days. Tell me what you're looking at."

"Dave, it's a wild trip. This is our senior assembly, right? Mr. Shott… he's up there? You see him, right?"

I looked to the front of the ballroom. Our senior class President, Mark Manetti, had just finished announcing the raffle winners. He did look a bit like our old principal, Mr. Shott. "That's not Mr. Shott, Joey. It's Mark Manetti."

"Oh, it *is* Mark. He looks just like Mr. Shott now. But Mr. Shott, he was there a minute ago."

"Why was Mr. Shott there a minute ago, Joey? What was he doing?"

"We were in the senior assembly on the last day of class, and I remember thinking, 'I wonder what this will look like thirty years from now.' The next thing I knew, I'm sitting here with all you guys and we're all old."

"Far out," I said.

"Yeah, it is. This room, our gym… It's like a time machine. We've all traveled forward in time. All of us. We were eighteen a second ago, now we're old. See that guy in the wheelchair over there? That's Larry Hopkins. He used to beat the shit out of me. Now he's got Parkinson's. And I'm not feeling sorry for him at all. I just want to go over and beat the shit out of *him*. And those football players at the table up front? They made fun of me when I did that concert at lunchtime in the cafeteria. Now they're fat old men."

I looked at the dance floor. Plump middle-aged people were doing the electric slide. "Joey, for what it's worth… I always thought you were the coolest kid in school. I'm sorry you're on a bad trip."

He stopped shaking his head and turned to me and smiled. "Thanks, man. You were always cool to me. But you know what? It didn't turn out the way I thought it would."

I looked around the room, reached over and patted Joey on the shoulder. "No, it didn't, Joey. It didn't, for hardly any of us."

I sat there with Joey for a while, squinting my eyes and trying to picture the people on the dance floor as they appeared at senior prom, but I couldn't make it happen. Gary appeared next to me. "There you are. I've had about enough. Are you ready to get out of here?"

"What do you say we get some breakfast?" Gary asked as we exited the ballroom. "There's a Waffle House right across the street." I hadn't been to a Waffle House in decades, but it had been one of our late-night haunts in high school.

The server brought menus and I declined, just ordering coffee. "Nonsense," Gary said. "You haven't eaten anything all evening. You're a mess, and after all the booze and weed you've been consuming, you need to eat something." He placed two orders for our usual from back in the day: a pecan waffle sandwich with a rasher of bacon as the filler, all drowned in Waffle House fake maple syrup.

"Here, drink this." He pushed my glass of water over to me. "I think you're dehydrated." I drank the entire glass of water, and he pushed his over to me as well and watched as I downed the second glass. When our food came, we ate silently, and even though I hadn't eaten since I'd had part of a Danish for breakfast, I still couldn't make a dent in the pile of food in front of me.

Gary put his fork down. "We need to talk," he said. "When were you going to tell me? Or were you going to tell me at all?"

"Tell you what?"

"Stop with the bullshit. You can't fool me. You're skin and bones. You have no appetite, and you're not acting like yourself. It's as if you're here on some *make amends mission* for Lisa Dahl."

"You were listening in?"

"You're damn right I was. I've been worried about you."

I was silent. I'd felt guilty about not telling him, but I just couldn't make myself.

"It must be bad," he said. "How long do you have?"

"A couple of months, maybe," I said, feeling relieved. "I'm foregoing treatment. I'm not going to live my last weeks being a science experiment when there's no reasonable expectation of a cure."

"I understand. I would feel the same way," he said. "But I don't understand this guilt trip you're on. You're a great guy. You've taken care of your kids, and you've been kind to your ex-wives."

I nodded. This was true, more or less. "But, don't you have regrets? Things you would have done differently?"

"Of course I do. Everyone does. It's called being human. Life is pretty much just stumbling from one mistake to another. Once in a while we get something right, and that needs to be enough. You've gotten many things right." He smiled. "You've been a great friend to me."

"I haven't been a great friend. You have been to me, though. I'd go months without returning your calls."

"Look," he said, "we live a thousand miles apart. You've had a complicated life. You most definitely do not owe me any kind of apology. And you don't owe one to Lisa either. She's been married for the last two decades and has a beautiful family." He frowned in the contemplative way I remembered so well and, in that moment, he looked sixteen again to me. "I can't imagine what you're going through. But I want you to know… I cherish our friendship. I mean that."

That night I slept better than I had in weeks. The next morning, Gary and I had brunch together and watched the Cleveland Browns get annihilated by the New York Giants in the hotel bar. When I left that afternoon, our hug was a little longer than when we'd arrived. There were no tears, but I told him I'd call him soon. I was pretty sure I meant it this time.

On the way out, I drove through downtown Canton for the last time, and now I didn't feel as sorry for my hometown. It had had its glorious moment in the sun, even a place in history, and that was enough. I pointed my car toward my daughter's home in Pennsylvania. I had a new grandson to meet.

Sign up for our newsletter and be the first to know when new Water Street Crime titles are released.

https://mailchi.mp/waterstreetpressbooks.com/ waterstreetcrimemailinglist

Get the Water Street Crime Starter Library FOR FREE

Get four, full-length ebooks – **BLOODY PARADISE, FROM ICE TO ASHES, TROPICAL ICE,** and **SING FOR THE DEAD** – and lots more exclusive content, all for free!

Building a relationship with our readers is the very best thing about publishing. We occasionally send newsletters with details on new releases, special offers and other bits of news relating to Water Street Press.

And if you sign up to the mailing list we'll send you all this free stuff:

1. A free ebook edition of the exotic thriller **BLOODY PARADISE** – "…a spicy thriller…"
2. A free ebook edition of the crime thriller **FROM ICE TO ASHES** – "designed to shoot the ice down your spine…"
3. A free ebook edition of the eco-thriller **TROPICAL ICE** – "…well-spun, tautly written…"
4. A free ebook edition of the delightfully noir-ish mystery **SING FOR THE DEAD** – Foreword Reviews' Gold Medal winner
5. Advance notice about the release of new Water Street Crime novels.

You can get all this and more, for free, just by signing up at
**https://mailchi.mp/waterstreetpressbooks.com/
waterstreetcrimemailinglist**

Did you enjoy this book? You can make a big difference for our amazing Water Street Crime authors.

Reviews are the most powerful tools in our arsenal when it comes to getting attention for our books. Much as we'd like to, we don't have the financial muscle of a New York publisher. We can't take out full-page ads in the newspaper or put posters on the subway.

(Not yet, anyway.)

But we do have something much more powerful and effective than that, and it's something that those publishers would kill to get their hands on.

A committed and loyal bunch of readers.

Honest reviews of our books help bring them to the attention of other readers.

If you've enjoyed this book we would be very grateful if you could spend just five minutes on Amazon or the online vendor of your choice leaving a review (it can be as short as you like).

Thank you very much.

ABOUT THE AUTHOR

Dennis D. Wilson is the author of The Dean Wister Series: the novels, *The Grand,* and *The Grand Prize,* and the short story collection, *The Grand Sextet.* After a career working in an international consulting firm and as a financial executive with two public companies, Dennis returns to the roots he established as a high school literature and writing teacher. His work draws upon his experiences from his hometown of Chicago, his years of living, working, hiking, and climbing in Jackson Hole, and secrets gleaned from time spent in corporate boardrooms, to craft political crime thrillers straight from today's headlines. Dennis lives in suburban Chicago with his wife and Black Lab Jenny, but spends as much time as he can, looking for adventure in the mountains and on his motorcycle. Keep up with him at **dennisdwilson.com**.

ALSO FROM WATER STREET PRESS

Ready for more thrills?

We suggest *Stained Fortune*, by Joe Calderwood, the
first in his Clint Kennedy Crime Series.

Have you read all the books in the Water Street Crime
collection? Check out Water Street Press at this link and
see all the amazing books we have to offer:
https://www.waterstreetpressbooks.com

A DEAN WISTER CRIME STORY, #1
THE GRAND
"Wilson crafts a classic crime thriller plot." Kirkus Reviews
DENNIS D. WILSON

Enjoy this excerpt from
THE GRAND,
the first book in the Dean Wister Series
by Dennis D. Wilson.

Chapter 1

enator Thomas McGraw sat back in the hand-dis-
tressed, buffalo-hide easy chair and contemplated
the room around him. This was his first visit to
the brand new, custom-designed mountain home of his
lover. When their affair started a little over a year ago,
what a sweet and savory surprise it had been to both of
them. A business relationship grew into friendship, and
then suddenly and unexpectedly exploded into something else – a red-hot, cross-country, obsessive romance
fueled by shared erotic tastes. The senator felt sexually
liberated under the spell of his exotic lover, and he was
pretty sure those feelings were mutual. True, they needed
to be discreet for a variety of reasons – indiscretion had
nearly cost them everything – but they had worked it
out. Although hectic schedules limited their rendezvous
to only a couple of weekends a month, the deprivation
and anxiety of anticipation made these weekends that

much more satisfying. He was generally in a frenzy by the time he could get to her.

The room was the den of a typical ten-thousand-square-foot vacation home of the rich and powerful in Jackson Hole, Wyoming. Decked out in nouveau western, its reclaimed timbers, Wyoming sandstone, and river rock were either complemented by – or detracted from, depending on your esthetic point of view – the original modern paintings depicting bold and most definitely non-earth-toned western landscapes and various forms of neon-colored wildlife. As Tom sipped his twenty-three-year-old Pappy Van Winkle, he studied the visage of a purple and orange moose head sculpted from California mahogany hanging dispiritedly over the fireplace. Damn, any self-respecting Wyoming moose would be embarrassed to know that this is some guy's idea of what a trophy moose should look like. His personal style was more traditional Western – big wooden beams and a glut of real dead animal heads on the walls. But, the sex was still new and novel, unlike anything he had felt before, and he was willing to overlook these stylistic differences for the time being or, who knew, maybe for a long time. As his mentor had told him a long time ago: "Pussy is a powerful motivator."

"I am soooo happy we were able to start our weekend a day early," his lover called from the other room. "I've been so horny this week that I've been bouncing off the walls. I brought back something special for you from

Chicago. Just give me another minute, sweetie." Charlotte Kidwell dressed, and undressed, to accentuate her best features: her big green eyes, her long, toned legs, and her perfect bubble butt. Her regular head-to-toe salon appointments, personal trainer, and strict dietary regimen were essentials to the healthy, put-together appearance that women of her age and social status often have, if they have the money and motivation to work at it. In her younger days, her insecure attempts to add sex appeal fell short, and she'd ended up with an oddly unfeminine look with her clumsy and unsuccessful experiments with cosmetics. But middle age had actually softened her features, and as she became more adept at the finer points of female grooming, she began to realize how much she resembled her sister. During what she referred to as "The Sexual Awakening," she had finally developed the confidence in her sexuality to consciously emulate her sister's makeup and dress. Her older sibling had always exuded effortless sexuality, and throughout high school and college had gone through more boys in most years than Charlotte had dated for her entire youth.

The senator had certainly surprised her. Although his belly professed his lust for food and drink and a disinclination for exercise, his face was the opposite, exuding an irresistible cowboy masculinity. At middle age, most people have to choose between a wrinkle-free face and a toned and youthful body. What was it her friend in Chicago called fat? "Nature's botox."

He had chosen his beautiful face at the expense of his body, but that was fine with her, because he was a sexual artiste. Certainly no one who knew him could possibly conceive of the hot spring of sexuality that was percolating beneath his surface. In spite of their distinctly different personalities, she considered him her soul mate. The first man in her forty-four years who had ever laid claim to that title. The thought made her giggle.

"Hurry up, baby, and get your pretty little ass out here."

Appearing in the doorway, she framed herself with the hand-on-the-hip pose so popular with women much younger than herself. "You like? I know this little specialty boutique in Chicago, and it ain't Macy's Intimate Apparel."

He liked the look very much. The red lace push-up bra, matching thong panties, silk kimono, and six-inch stilettos appealed to the man who'd had a weakness for strippers in his younger days. Though the untied robe looked more like a cape than boudoir attire, and the entire outfit reminded him of a porn movie he once saw – Superslut, a parody of Superwoman, he had to give her an "A" for effort. "Wow, you look like a very sexy Little Red Riding Hood. And where in the world did you find a bra that makes those pretty little A cups of yours look like Cs? Now turn around and let me admire your world-class bootie."

She did a little twirl for him, grinned, and pushed together her bra cups to emphasize her cleavage. "It's called a miracle bra, and see, it does work miracles. Now you just sit there and sip your whiskey. I have another surprise for you." She strutted over to the bookcase, flipped a switch, and AC/DC's "Shook Me All Night Long" filled the room. And she began to dance.

"Oh my." Tom took a big swallow and relished the burn. "You are just full of surprises tonight."

"Just sit back and enjoy, Senator. I've got a few more surprises coming your way."

Watching her rehearsed moves, the familiar hunger began to stir below his opulent belly. And then, in a maneuver that would have been impressive for a woman of any age, she turned away from him, spread her legs, touched her toes, looked straight up at him from her bare inverted V, and twerked. She had been practicing all afternoon, and when she saw the image of her quivering butt in the mirror she couldn't wait to see his reaction.

"Oh, my god, where did you learn that?" The stirring rising now to a different level. And he was also wondering... her dance routine looked really professional.

"I have a very good friend in Chicago who does this for a living, and she's been giving me some lessons."

"Judging from that pose, sweetie, your friend must be an instructor in 'stripper yoga'." The senator, feeling the fire down there, leaned forward and reached for that perfect ass. "Get over here and let me take you the way

I like, the way I know you like." Putting his hands on her bare cheeks and grabbing two hands full, he left his chubby fingerprints as indentations on her flesh. Crazed now, pulling off his pants and underwear but not bothering with his shirt and tie, he pulled her thong aside, mounted her, grunting, sighing. Both of them grunting, sighing, grunting some more. And now just the sounds of flesh slapping flesh. And AC/DC, urging them on...

Hayden Smith was running late. He was always running late. It was common knowledge in town that you had to book every appointment with Hayden an hour early to get him to show up on time. Attorney, county commissioner, real estate broker and developer, owner of a property management company – all that, plus trying to live up to the moniker of Teton County's most eligible bachelor as determined by Mountain Woman magazine, well, that could take a toll on a man, even a man as fit and athletic as Hayden. And it was taking its toll on Hayden today. Sometimes he thought there was little point in taking any time off because you had to work twice as hard just to clear your schedule.

The last item of the day on his long list was to make sure all was in order in the home of his newest property management client before their arrival the next morning. But what he really was thinking about, as he put the key in the door, was that he was already an hour late for a dinner date at the home of one of Teton County's richest and most beautiful socialites. And so if he hadn't been fantasizing about the evening's upcoming sensual activities, and if he hadn't assumed that it was his cleaning crew that had left that open bourbon bottle on the counter, and if he hadn't been formulating the words he was going to use to chew Pablo's ass about getting control of his maintenance team, and if he had checked his voicemail after his last two meetings instead of engaging in licentious banter on the phone with the young socialite, then he might have reacted differently to the pounding bass of one of the most iconic rock anthems of the 1980s. He might not have followed the mesmerizing sound of Brian Johnson's sandpaper voice into the den, assuming that he would find some of his employees having an unauthorized party; and he might not have witnessed the sight in front of him that would not only drastically change his life but would also set in motion a chain of events that had the potential to change the course of American history.

If he had looked directly at the man's face, he almost certainly would have recognized one of the most well-known faces in Wyoming, soon to be equally famous throughout America. However, Hayden looked everywhere but into his face. The man, still dressed for business on top but naked from the waist down, was humping a pretty redhead doggie style, and Hayden was fascinated that with each thrust, her red stilettos would come off the ground about twelve inches, and then at the end of the thrust, the tips of her heels would bang down on the pine floor. Thrust, bang, thrust, bang, thrust, bang. Later when he played that video clip back in his mind, he captioned it "porn star tap dancing."

He looked all around the room, but his eyes kept coming back to those red shoes, maybe because he didn't really want to look at the man's jiggling ass, or maybe because when his eyes followed those shoes north he was treated to a pair of the finest legs and most delicious bootie that he had ever seen. If he had been thinking clearly, he would have just turned around and walked right out of the house and he would have been able to go back to his great life as Teton County's busiest and most eligible bachelor. But for whatever reason – the shock of the scene, or his own perverse voyeurism – he did not turn back around. He knocked on the door jamb with his clipboard and stammered loudly enough to be heard over AC/DC. "Ah, ah, ah, I thought you weren't coming in until tomorrow. I just came to check on the house. Is everything OK? I mean, just call me if anything isn't OK. Sorry to interrupt. I'll just let myself out..." And then he backed out of the room and nearly sprinted out the door.

Tom jumped up with impressive agility considering his exertion and girth, partly hopping, definitely bobbing. "Oh shit, oh shit, oh shit."

Charlotte rolled over onto her side. "What the fuck, I left him a message that I was coming in today. What was he thinking?"

And the senator just kept repeating, "Oh, shit, oh, shit, oh, shit." Then, catching his breath, added to his mantra, "I'm sure he saw me, I'm sure he saw me, I'm sure he saw me."

His lover, handing him the rest of his twenty-three-year-old Pappy, said, "Here, drink this," trying not to let the panic sound in her voice. She thought for a moment. "We'll call Mario. He'll know what to do. If that asshole tells anyone it'll hurt Mario as much as us. Well, maybe not quite as much as us, but you know what I mean."

Tom sat down for a minute, his white dress shirt soaked through, wheezing from the exertion, from the excitement, from the fear, his heart a thumping kettle drum in his chest. Neither of them said a word for a minute, then two. Finally realizing the heart attack wasn't coming, he took a huge breath and said, "OK, call him."

Charlotte punched the number into her mobile phone. "Mario? Sorry to bother you, but we have a problem. Some asshole just walked in on the two of us. Walked in on us… you know. What do you think we were doing? How could he not recognize him? Yeah, he's my property manager. Hold on. Honey, would you hand me that business card on the table?"